Theodore Russell Monro

Love Lost, But Honour Won

A novel. Part 2

Theodore Russell Monro

Love Lost, But Honour Won
A novel. Part 2

ISBN/EAN: 9783337048556

Printed in Europe, USA, Canada, Australia, Japan

Cover: Foto ©Andreas Hilbeck / pixelio.de

More available books at **www.hansebooks.com**

LOVE LOST, BUT HONOUR WON.

A Novel.

BY

THEODORE RUSSELL MONRO,

AUTHOR OF 'THE VANDELEURS OF RED TOR,' ETC.

IN THREE VOLUMES.
VOL. II.

London:

SAMUEL TINSLEY & CO.,

10 SOUTHAMPTON STREET, STRAND.

1878.

CONTENTS OF VOL. II.

CHAP.   PAGE

   I. ANNE BRASSINGHAM SPEAKS HER MIND .   1

  II. LADY AMORY THINKS IT TIME TO IN-
     TERFERE 17

  III. MOTHER AND SON 31

  IV. THE HEIR AND HIS ELDER BROTHER . 40

   V. DICK FERRIS, THE WILLESDEN CHICKEN . 57

  VI. MADAME FERRAND SEEKS ASSISTANCE . 76

  VII. GEORGE FERRIS RECOGNIZES HIS MOTHER 99

VIII. MR. WILLIAM CAVEY LAYS A TRAIN . 110

  IX. MADAME FERRAND TAKES SERVICE AT
     BRASSINGHAM 118

   X. THE VEREKER FAMILY 127

  XI. EXPLAINS THE POSITION OF AFFAIRS AT
     BRASSINGHAM 133

  XII. CONCERNING THE BRASSINGHAM DIAMONDS 146

  XIII. A WATER-PARTY 158

  XIV. THEODORA PADDLES HER OWN CANOE . 174

  XV. FERRAND AND FREEMAN . . . 184

  XVI. "WHEN GREEK MEETS GREEK, THEN COMES
     THE TUG OF WAR" 203

  XVII. THE RIVALS 216

XVIII. FERRAND AND FERRIS . . . 229

  XIX. ALICE RETURNS MISS CHAMPNEYS'S CALL 235

LOVE LOST, BUT HONOUR WON.

CHAPTER I.

ANNE BRASSINGHAM SPEAKS HER MIND.

By breakfast-time the following morning the news of Mr. Vereker's engagement to Miss Brassingham, and Mr. Brassingham's to Miss Champneys had permeated the whole mass of visitors to the Wells. The first had for some days past been looked upon as an accomplished fact, but the announcement of the second came like a thunder-clap not only on society generally, but even on the members of Mr. Brassingham's own family, by one and all of whom, as may readily be imagined, it was listened to with extremest disfavour.

Anne Brassingham especially was furious that that "chit of a child," as she called Violet, should be promoted to her mother's vacant place; and Theodora, though from different reasons, was equally angry at her father's senseless infatuation and Violet's subtle manœuvring, for in such lights did the conduct of each appear to her under the present circumstances. Besides, Theodora had strong reasons of her own for believing that Violet's heart was in Charlie's keeping; and in her chivalrous desire always to protect the interests of the absent she found another reason for objecting to what seemed like stealing a march upon her brother.

Perhaps none of the ladies of the Brassingham family cared very much what line the head of the house chose to pursue so far as they themselves were concerned. Anne would be Mrs. Vereker before Violet became Mrs. Brassingham; May's heart was too full to the brim of love's young dream for Eric Amory to let anybody else's love affairs cause her any serious concern; and aunt

Lavinia had her own fish to fry with the Reverend Silas Monckton.

But Anne was jealous for her dead mother's sake, as Theodora was jealous for the sake of her absent brother, and although the latter was too large-hearted to allow herself to be prejudiced against Violet simply because she would be her stepmother, and rule in Mr. Brassingham's house to her own exclusion, still she felt a scornful contempt for a girl who, while loving one man, could allow herself to be engaged to another; and where Theodora had formed estimates of character in her own mind we know she was never shy of disburdening her thoughts with some strength of diction to all and any who might care to listen.

The three girls were alone together in their private sitting-room on the morning of the day on which the two engagements had been announced to the world at large, and the subject of discussion was, very naturally, their father's marriage.

"I should not have minded so much,"

Theodora was saying, "if Charlie had but been here to hold his own, if there is anything of his own to hold, but it seems to me so mean of papa to have brought Violet away from Charlie's influence on purpose to get the field free for himself. I hate meanness!"

"All is fair in love and war," observed Anne, sententiously.

"Which is only one of the false and wicked proverbs that ought to be rooted out of the language of any civilized state," rejoined Theodora.

"I do not think you can accuse papa of meanness, Theodora," observed May, thoughtfully. "He has certainly given Mr. Ferrand a fair chance with Violet ever since we came here, and Violet's conduct with that man goes very far to prove she cannot have cared very much for Charlie."

"I don't agree with you at all," said Theodora decisively. "Violet is terrified by Mr. Ferrand. She is not in love with him; and, indeed, in a place like this, I do not see how a girl is to avoid a man's persecutions unless she gives him the cut direct."

"Violet is a scheming little minx," said Anne. "She only wanted to bring papa to the point, and encouraged Mr. Ferrand's attentions as the most sure way of doing so."

"For my part," said May, "the idea of a marriage between papa and Violet had never even entered my head. He has always had a gentle, fatherly manner towards her—more fatherly than he uses to any of his own children—but this news has quite taken my breath away. You, at any rate, Anne, will not have to clash with her. I suppose you will take care to be married to Vere before we are honoured with the presence of a young stepmother."

"In a month from the present time," said Anne decisively, "I hope to have done with the old life, and I advise you both to follow my example with all convenient speed. It has always been bad enough to

have to put up with papa's violent temper
and dictatorial ways, and I certainly don't
envy you having to play second fiddle to
that little soft cat, Violet, as the future Mrs.
Brassingham ! "

" I dare say the situation will be as toler-
able as having to eat 'humble pie' per-
petually to Vere's maiden aunts," said
Theodora, whose back was getting up at
Anne's abuse of their father. " I expect
you will find them even more trying than
your own family, Anne."

" I quite expect it will be war to the
knife with them both," answered Anne,
doggedly, " and I am quite prepared for
them and it. Open warfare has a charm of
its own which only blossoms into full flower
when waged with one's consort's family; but
that sort of petty skirmishing which goes on
in the bosom of one's own family, and which is
checked, now by duty, now by a half-hearted
affection, and now by fear of the con-
sequences to one's own peace, is a much
more disagreeable form of conflict."

" Those Misses Vereker are such awful old
cats, though," said May; " and I suppose
you will be obliged to be decently civil to
them, as Vere's future prospects depend
entirely on how they leave their money.
Then there is the bachelor uncle, too. · I
have heard that he is almost worse than his
sisters! Well, Anne, I do hope you will
be happy."

" Thank you, my dear; I hope so too,"
answered Anne, with some asperity, for she
was thoroughly alive to the doubt implied
by her sister's congratulations as to the
wisdom of her choice. " As I have made my
bed so I must lie on it, and I dare say Vere
and I will shake down into matrimony with
as few jars as most folks. And now that we
are on the subject of marriage," added
Anne, with that cow-like awkwardness that
was one of her chief characteristics, both of
body and mind, " it is high time, my dears,
that you made up your minds which of you
means to be Mrs. Eric Amory; for the man's
attentions to you both have set the whole

establishment on the *qui vive* as to which
he really means to honour with his prefer-
ence!"

Oh, is there any mischief-maker on earth
the equal of a stupid woman? Anne had
no tact, no discretion, no sensitiveness; her
mental hide was as tough as that of a
rhinoceros, and her remark, made not with
any malice aforethought, but a natural out-
come of the gross stupidity of her nature,
went clean home to the passionate hearts of
both her sisters—hearts, alas! beating to
one common throb, the pulse of love; beating for one mortal man, who, attracted by
both, could not divorce himself from the
society of either, and had raised hopes in
the minds of each which to one of the two
at least must bring—a broken heart!

May flushed crimson at Anne's words, and
Theodora became pale as death. May moved
to the window and plucked some leaves of
the Virginia creeper which nodded in at
the casement, trying to conceal the confusion
and blushes with which Anne's amazing

dulness of comprehension had covered her; but Theodora, though the shaft had gone straight home, was cast in a different mental mould to May. She was a woman who could suffer and be strong, and after the first sharp pang of jealousy had passed, her instinct was rather to guard her sister's secret than her own. For Theodora possessed the protecting instincts of a lover rather than the confiding helplessness of a girl beloved. Her very passion for Eric was rather of a masculine than a feminine nature. Strong men had wooed her and had failed; wise men had laid their secrets open to her ken, but without success; rich men had poured out their treasures at her feet, and had returned discomfited; beauty and intellect and wealth, all had entered the lists for this queenly woman, and all had failed, for her heart was filled with but one image, that of a curly-headed, blue-eyed boy, on whose lips the down had scarcely strengthened, on whose fresh, fair young face time had not yet effaced the dimples, on whose broad, smooth

brow care had as yet engraved no line.
But, strong as her love was for Eric Amory,
it had not blinded her resolute common sense,
nor had she allowed it to stifle the protecting
love she had always felt for her youngest
sister. At this moment she felt the imperious
necessity of standing in the breach, and
saving May from making unmaidenly confession of her heart's best hopes.

The colour slowly returned to her cheeks
as she replied, with an assumed disdain,—

"Birds in their little nests agree, my dear
Anne, and Eric having been a little bird
brought up in our nest for so many years, a
close intimacy is to be looked for with all of
us; one cannot be supposed to marry all the
little boys one has played puss-in-the-corner
with in one's infancy. People may make
what surmises they please, as far as May and
I are concerned."

"I am glad to hear it," said Anne, with
much dignity. "It is a great relief to my
mind, for of course you will understand now
that I shall move in such a different set from

heretofore that I should be very glad if you both married somebody—well—somebody rather better born than the grandson of a dolls'-eye manufacturer!"

"For the matter of that," said Theodora, firing up, and taken entirely off her guard, "I don't see that the grandson of a dolls'-eye maker is any worse than the granddaughter of an overseer on an iron mine, who couldn't spell words of two syllables· correctly up to his dying day."

"My dear, you need not blaspheme your ancestors, even to vindicate the aristocracy of that pretty boy to whose attractions you do not seem so insensible as you would have us believe. Ah, what would not we swarthy Brassinghams give for a complexion of milk and roses like Eric Amory's! It's a shame it should have been wasted on a man," added she, as she languidly gazed at her own dark skin in the glass. "However, I do not think Vere is aware whether I am black or white, so perhaps after all it does not very much signify."

"Have you fixed your wedding day, Anne?" asked May from the window, rushing at the chance of turning the conversation back into a less dangerous channel.

"Yes! the first of October is fixed," answered her sister; "and we are to return to Brassingham at the end of this week, partly to make arrangements for my wedding, partly to introduce Violet to the neighbourhood as the future Mrs. Brassingham, and partly from some new anxiety papa feels about Charlie, who seems to be 'hand and glove' with a rather rougher lot than usual."

"How do you know?" asked Theodora, defiantly, for she was ever ready to do battle for her brother, especially with Anne.

"I saw a letter written to Mr. Monckton, who has been making inquiries for papa and aunt Lavinia."

"Meddling little prig!" said Theodora, in a loud aside.

"Pray don't be abusive, Theodora," con-

tinued Anne, " Mr. Monckton has only done
as he was asked, and, as there seems to be
every chance of his becoming our uncle by
marriage, we may as well treat him with
civility, even behind his back."

" But what about Charlie ?" asked May
impatiently from the window.

"Charlie seems to have taken up his
quarters with some people who are strongly
suspected of being receivers of stolen
goods," answered Anne, with much lofty
contempt. " Fond of low society as our
brother is, I did give him credit for having
enough sense to keep on the right side of
the law. While he only affected the society
of prize-fighters, jockeys, and acrobats,
there was not much harm done to any one
but himself, but it is quite a different matter
now. I wonder what the Verekers would
say if they had any inkling of what sort of
a brother-in-law Vere was to have ! "

" I don't believe one word of that sleek
old Puritan's information," said Theodora,
hotly. " Of course it is possible that

Charlie may have acquaintances who are rough characters, perhaps more than rough, but I will never believe that his companions are people whom he knows to be dishonest. What earthly reason Mr. Monckton can have for blackening Charlie's character to his own father is more than I can divine, but papa seems more than willing to believe anything to Charlie's discredit just now. Perhaps the parson thought tale-bearing might curry favour, and pave the way to his addresses to aunt Lavinia being favourably entertained by the head of the house."

"I do not fancy aunt Lavinia is the person to ask any mortal man what she shall or what she shall not do," answered Anne. "She is a Brassingham to the core, obstinate and combative, and if she means to marry the Reverend Silas she will do so without papa's consent, you may be very sure. But to return to our muttons. These people, with whom Charlie is, beyond a doubt, in constant and close intercourse, do bear a very bad name. The house is an old ram-shackle place, far from any high road, half inn, half farm, kept by a man called Ferris, a retired prize-fighter. Mr. Monckton has found out that a very motley crew resort to this place, not only the best-known pugilists, wrestlers, and others of that class, but young men who are being trained for special distances in foot-races, and gentlemen who have reasons for wishing to keep dark for a time and yet to be in the immediate vicinity of London."

" Still, these are not the sort of people who consort with thieves or receivers of stolen goods," urged Theodora.

" There have been several burglaries in the neighbourhood lately," answered Anne, " and several persons who have been seen at Ferris's are suspected by the police. At any rate the reports that have reached papa of Charlie's associates are sufficiently alarming to have made him decide on going back to Surrey at once. But I hear Vere's voice outside. I will go down to him; and if there are any little affairs to settle before leaving the Wells," she added, significantly, as she left the room, " there is no time to lose, for I know we shall be gone before the week is out."

CHAPTER II.

LADY AMORY THINKS IT TIME TO INTERFERE.

BOTH Lady Amory and Mrs. Higgins had by this time quite understood that they neither of them were in the betting for the first place in Mr. Brassingham's affections. Nevertheless each felt a secret satisfaction at the discomfiture of the other's too palpable plans for becoming the second Mrs. Brassingham, and although, in their eagerness to avail themselves of the off-chance, they had both unceremoniously thrown the parson over into the very arms of Miss Lavinia, nevertheless that each should have failed was some compensation to the other.

Although Mrs. Higgins had set her cap at

Mr. Brassingham in vain, she still was
determined to let no opportunity slip of
improving her acquaintance with the family.
Perhaps, though the father had escaped her,
the son might fall an easy prey to the
freckled charms of her daughter. Who
could tell?

So Mrs. Higgins determined to make
hay while the sun shone, and cast about for
any links which might rivet her acquaintance with the Brassinghams, and place her
on an equal footing with a family who
thought nothing of snubbing her whenever
she pressed her friendliness into familiarity.

In the fast alliance between Agatha Bonchurch and Theodora, Mrs. Higgins found
ground for hope, also in the fact that both
Vere and Anne owed her daughter something for the self-sacrificing way in which
she had constituted herself gooseberry-
picker on countless occasions.

Then Mr. Brassingham liked the Tempests; that was evident. She would herself

ask the Tempests to pay her a visit at
Barnes at the end of September. The
Tempests would, of course, be asked to
Anne Brassingham's wedding, and then it
would be quite impossible for the Tempests'
hostess to be disregarded in the invitation.
If the Tempests, why, of course, Captain
Selfe and Mr. Ferrand must be asked as
well; and as to Loftus, Mrs. Higgins was
not the sort of person to mind much about
any man's taking a glass too much, if by
receiving him as her guest she could gain
any point she had in view.

So the Tempests were asked with their
satellites, and Mrs. Higgins's invitation was
accepted with graciousness, and even alac-
rity; for Mrs. Tempest's account at her
banker's was dwindling to the uttermost
farthing, while Captain Selfe had let his
gambling talents lie idle, for lack of pigeons
to pluck, ever since he had been vegetating
at the Wells.

Ferrand was only too glad to accept any
invitation which would give him a chance of

seeing Violet; for although he was utterly
astounded and bewildered at the turn affairs
had taken, still he clung to his forlorn hope
that something might interfere with Mr.
Brassingham's marriage to Violet, with all
the tenacity of purpose that was so instinct
in his determined nature.

Mr. Brassingham had given his daughters
to understand that he meant to be married
himself immediately after Anne had become
Mrs. Vereker. He seemed pleased rather
than otherwise that his eldest daughter
should have chosen as she had. The Verekers were thoroughly well connected, and
the son of the iron-founder was more than
content that his daughters should find admittance into the houses of the English aristocracy.

Vere's career had all along been hampered
by poverty alone. He was clever, steady,
and well born. With Anne's inheritance to
back him up, he might aim at and achieve
almost any position. The Verekers were an
old county family, whose sons had done

their country good service both in the field
and in the legislature, and whose daughters
in every generation had intermarried with
sons of the nobility.

What was to prevent Vere being returned
for a division of his county? Visions of an
M.P. for a son-in-law were not unpleasant
to Mr. Brassingham, though he affected a
contempt for all social distinctions no
Englishman, however great a Radical he
may be, ever really and truly feels.

Beyond Mr. Brassingham's liking for the
match on such grounds as these, it seemed
to him a special providence that took Anne
into another family before he made Violet
the mistress of his own home. Theodora's
strong good sense would not allow her to
throw causeless difficulties in the way of a
young wife, and May was naturally too
amiable to quarrel with a girl of Violet's
gentle temper; but Mr. Brassingham had
had a long experience of what his eldest
daughter was capable of in her powers of
being disagreeable, and it may be supposed

he was not sorry that Violet should be spared so great an infliction.

Mr. Brassingham had himself asked Lady Catherine and her son Frank to stay at Brassingham Park for Anne's marriage, and Mr. Tresilian was to be Vere's best man. At aunt Lavinia's especial request, Mr. Monckton had been asked to perform the ceremony, there not being a parson in either the Vereker or the Brassingham family, and thus all the *côterie* that had been formed at the Wells would have an opportunity of improving each others' acquaintance among the hills and dales of Surrey. The Amorys, living on Wimbledon Common, were within easy distance also of both the Brassinghams and Higginses, and Lady Amory. however much she had failed in securing Mr. Brassingham's hand, felt no doubt as to her family being included in the marriage festivities. She was sorely puzzled, however, as to which of the Brassingham girls it was who was most favoured by her bright-eyed boy; while, on the other hand, she saw

mischief in the future from his inability
to make up his mind between them. Eric
never spoke of Theodora but in terms of
unmeasured admiration. Her wit, her
beauty, her sense, her daring, were themes
of which he never tired, and he was at as
little pains to conceal the admiration in his
eyes as on his tongue. Of May, on the
contrary, he seldom or never spoke at all,
yet when he spoke *to* her, his every word
was an implied caress. Lady Amory began
to feel that, for every one's sake, this vacil-
lation on Eric's part must cease. Had the
Brassinghams' mother been living, or had
their father been a little more sensitive to
the remarks which had been freely made at
the Wells about Eric's attentions to his two
younger daughters, there never could have
been any reason for her interference. But
Mr. Brassingham was too engrossed in his
own passion for Violet to care what his
daughters said or did, or what was said of
them; so Lady Amory, who, though weak
and vain, was in the main a kind-hearted

little woman, determined to put a decided
stop to Eric's double flirtation.

"My dear boy," said she to her son, on
the very morning of the announcement of
the two engagements, "there seems to be
much marrying and giving in marriage just
now in the Brassingham family. May I
ask which of the remaining young ladies
you think of presenting to me as a daughter-
in-law; for really, Eric," she added, more
seriously, "you are carrying on so
strong a flirtation with both May and
Theodora, that I am afraid the girls themselves do not know which of them it is
you prefer."

"Indeed, mother," answered Eric, laughing, "they cannot be more puzzled than
I. Most men fall in love with one woman
at a time, at any rate, even though they
may be 'to one thing constant never'; but
I, who care just now for no others on the
face of the earth but May and Theodora,
cannot for the life of me make up my mind
which of the two I do prefer. I wish

I were a Turk or a Mormon, and then I would marry them both."

Lady Amory was not the sort of woman to have any affectation in her manner towards her own son, nor was she one to profess being shocked at levity of expression, which she rated at its true worth—or worthlessness; but at this speech of her son's, laughingly as it was spoken, an expression of deep gravity and concern came over her face, and she spoke with an earnestness that was quite unusual to her.

"I do not like to hear you speak thus lightly of the matter, Eric. What is play to you may be death to others; and you do not seem to care how deeply you may wound. Besides, my dear boy, the choice of a wife is not the light matter you seem to think. That you should care so much for both only shows me that you are not honestly in love with either."

"Oh, that's the way all women talk!" returned Eric. "Just because a woman cannot be in love with two men at the same time, the sex denies that a man can care for more than one woman at a time."

"It is not only very unjust to women, Eric, if your remark were true, but it does not say much for the men," replied his mother.

"Well, mother, I dare say we are a very poor lot, but that does not alter the fact that a man may be in love with two women at the same time, and unable to make up his mind which he wants to marry. I admire Theodora the most, but I am a little afraid of her, and she is of so jealous a temperament I should be afraid to speak to other women after we were married, which, you know, mother, would hardly suit my book," he added, laughing. "May would make a charming little wife, and I do love her immensely; but sometimes she says such ridiculously silly things—partly from her youth, and partly from inexperience—that she makes one shudder at the possibility of the future Mrs. Amory making such blunders in society."

"I have no pity for you, Eric," said his

mother. " The time will come when you will know the pain of love. At present you are hardly even sipping its mildest pleasures; but, as I said before, what is play to you is death to others. The Brassinghams are motherless girls, and May, at any rate, is very young—indeed, has seen, as yet, absolutely nothing of the world—therefore, Eric, if you are not in earnest about either of them, carry your bow and arrows elsewhere, and do not disturb their peace. If they had been more women of the world than they are, my son, they would have paid you out by leading you on and fooling you to the top of your bent, and then coolly throwing you over as soon as you had lost your heart and your head. But they are both good, unaffected, true-hearted girls, Eric, either of whom I would gladly welcome as your wife; and although I do not wish to interfere more than I must with your flirtations, I think matters are growing serious with them, if not with you; and I cannot stand by silent and hear you called a heartless flirt."

" My dear mother," said Eric, amazed at
so earnest a reproof from his usually flighty
parent; " indeed you take this matter much
too seriously. We have been brought up
together for years. We flirted when we
were all babies together; surely there is no
reason to become cold and distant simply
because we have all come to the age when
most folks marry. I am very very fond of
both of them, and if I thought either of
them had suffered by fault of mine, I would
ask her to marry me out of hand to-
morrow."

" Do nothing rashly, Eric. To ask a girl
to marry you because you have made her
love you, may be chivalrous, but it is not
common sense. She must inevitably find out,
sooner or later, that you married her from a
sense of duty rather than from love, and
that knowledge will gall her to her dying
day, and poison all the fountains of her
otherwise possible happiness in life. Rather
break with her utterly, while she may turn
to another who may love her more worthily,

than bring a life-long misery upon both by
feigning a passion which you do not feel, in
order that you may satisfy the demands of
an exaggerated sense of honour."

"All right, mother," answered Eric, gravely
at last. "I certainly had not thought that
any harm could have come of my regard for
both the sisters; but I will be more on my
guard for the future as to my manner of
showing it. Indeed I am not vain enough
to suppose that such girls as the Brassinghams can have more than a friendly fancy
for me, as I have always had for them ; but I
will try to remember we are no longer
children, and tune my ways to greater
decorum."

"Any sudden change of manner will do
more harm than good, Eric. Keep away
from all serious subjects with them both for
the short time longer they remain at the
Wells, and when you all meet again at
Wimbledon, there will be enough excitement of other sorts, first with Anne's
wedding and then with Violet's, to keep

your young brains busy with other matters
than love-making. And now, my dear boy,
that I have cleared my conscience, do not
let me keep you from any amusement of the
hour. It is not often that I am given to
lecturing you. Grown-up people must have
toys as well as children. Happy are those
who have not a passion for edged tools."

CHAPTER III.

MOTHER AND SON.

At the hour and place appointed Julian Ferrand met his mother on this same morning. That lady had passed but a restless night. Trained as she had ever been in all the arts of dissimulation, and closely as she had always hidden in her own breast the sad story of her earlier years, yet she found it well-nigh impossible to plan her course upon the present occasion.

She had ever carefully hidden from both her sons the fact of their illegitimacy ; and even if one or both of them guessed that some mystery enveloped the circumstances of their birth, yet by no possible means, as far as she knew, could they have the remotest inkling of their connexion with the Brassinghams.

That her brother Ferris, the ex-prize-fighter, and his wife would hold their tongues on the matter she was certain. It was too greatly to their own interest to deny their connexion with Mr. Brassingham's cast-off mistress. The unsuccessful attempts to obtain the Brassingham diamonds had effectually stopped their mouths.

That Ferris had some reason for encouraging Charles Brassingham in remaining at the out-of-the-way farm-house, and in his intimacy with her own son George, she had no doubt; that the half-brothers should feel so strong an attachment to one another was no less unreasonable than their close resemblance in appearance. George Ferris had been adopted by his uncle, in consideration of certain money payments made by his mother to her brother, and had therefore been entirely separated from Julian, who had been educated abroad, and, until of late years, had seldom quitted his mother or the Bohemian sets in which she moved.

Mrs. Julia Ferris was greatly exercised in her mind as to whether the time had come when she should confide to both her sons their true birth and parentage. When by the brook she had seen Julian's earnest passion for a girl who might turn out to be one of Mr. Brassingham's own daughters, she had felt a sudden thrill of horror at the misery she might unwittingly have caused by withholding the truth from Julian; but when she knew that Violet Champneys was the object of her son's love, the old shrinking from exposing herself to the possible contempt of her own children returned in strong force and kept her silent. Of what use to give her sons the pain of knowing themselves bastards, or herself the agony of confession to a sinful past of which her sons had not the least suspicion? No; she would leave matters as they were, and carry her secret to the grave.

So when Julian made his appearance at

the rendezvous she had determined to tell him nothing of the truth, but to account for her mysterious presence in Yorkshire by any commonplace explanation which might come readiest to her mind and lips.

With her usual decision of character she went straight to her point on Julian's arrival.

"You must be much surprised," she said, "to find me here in Yorkshire, when you believed me to be still in Vienna. You know my sudden fancies for an entire change of scene; I longed to see England once more; the longing was so strong that I came straight away and only arrived in London less than a week ago. I had known Wharfdale in days before your birth, Julian, and I longed to revisit the scenes of my youth. I had been wandering through some of my old haunts, when I happened upon you yesterday by the side of the stream; and now tell me, Julian, how fares your love for this Miss Champneys, who, you tell me, is a ward of a Mr. Brassingham?"

"Mother," answered Julian, gravely, "I have loved that girl from the first moment I saw her, I do love her still with the whole strength and force of my nature; but all is changed since yesterday. Then I had hope; now I have none. That rivals should exist elsewhere was only natural, considering Violet's wondrous beauty and attractiveness, but at the Wells I saw no possible suitor for her hand. All the other men seemed to find greater charms in others than in her, and I was beginning to believe myself the favoured one, till suddenly to-day, but a few hours ago, Mr. Brassingham himself gave out that his ward was shortly to become his wife!"

Mrs. Ferris started back as though struck by some sudden blow. Her dark face grew white to the very lips. Then, by a strong effort regaining her composure, she said, in a low, firm voice,—

"Take heart, my son; Miss Champneys shall never be Mr. Brassingham's wife."

With such concentrated energy were the

words forced through her half-closed lips that
Julian stood silent in amazement. Her dark
eyes flashed out furiously from under her
heavy brows; her hands were interlaced in
some strong agony of emotion; her breath
came short and quick. Should she tell
him ?

Should she confide in him the secret of
her life ?

Should she confess to her own son that the
man who was his rival was no other than his
own father? that the place Violet Champneys sought to occupy should by rights have
been her own, and should be her own yet if
any power on earth could give it her? Who
so fitting as Mr. Brassingham's bastard son
to be made an accomplice in the mother's
designs to become Mr. Brassingham's lawful
wife? And yet, no; the mother's heart
hesitated, wavered, drew back, lest the son's
honourable soul should be tempted to dis-
honour, and again lest either or any of
those she loved so passionately should suffer
through a hasty and ill-advised disclosure.

No; she would wait. If scheme she must, she would scheme alone, and not force the taint of deception upon her son.

" Julian," she added presently, her fingers interlacing nervously as she continued, " you have ever found me a fond mother, have you not? and if hard in my dealings with the outside world, at least you will bear me witness that I have fought hard and worked hard that you might escape the necessity of any unfitting or uncongenial toil. Yes; I know you are grateful," she added, as with a wave of her hand she deprecatingly refused the caress with which he would have sealed his witness. " But now listen to me. Are you utterly in earnest about this auburn-haired girl—this Violet Champneys? I conjecture she is poor, even to dependence on Mr. Brassingham. Is it not so?"

" She is absolutely penniless, mother, and dependent on Mr. Brassingham. She told me so herself, but I love her with all my heart and soul and mind and strength."

" Enough, my son, I am satisfied. When

a nature so strong as yours loves thus it
will carry all before it."

"Unless, mother, she has given her heart
elsewhere."

"Is it to Mr. Brassingham you imagine
she has lost her heart?" said his mother,
scornfully.

"No, mother, certainly not to him, and
that is my ground for hope. Mr. Brassingham seems to me a man whom many a
woman might worship, but Violet Champneys has no sort of love for him save gratitude."

"Then, Julian, do not fret; Mr. Brassingham shall never marry her. Leave all
to me. All I require of you is implicit
obedience to my commands, however strange
they may appear. The day shall come when
Violet shall be not only willing but eager to
accept your love and bear your name.
Keep near her—in the same neighbourhood.
When do they return to Wimbledon?"

"At once, mother, and I shall not be far
from there. The Higginses, who live at

Barnes, have asked me to be their guest during the coming month. Their house is within a mile or two, I hear, of Brassingham Park."

"Good!" said his mother. "Strengthen whatever hold upon the girl you may already have by every means in your power. To-morrow I return to London. I shall be near at hand. If I send for you, come instantly; if I send a message, obey implicitly. Should you meet me, remember me no longer as your mother, but only as Giulia Ferretti, the actress, who won renown abroad, and whom you knew merely in that capacity. One thing more—no one knows we have met, let our meeting remain secret; I have my reasons. Later on, perhaps, you shall know all—not now."

Then they parted, and Julian Ferrand, whose lion heart was soft with a tender yearning love, such as never before had set his pulses throbbing, strode homeward to the Wells.

CHAPTER IV.

THE HEIR AND HIS ELDER BROTHER.

In the courtyard of Richard Ferris's house stood two young men, so marvellously alike that a stranger would have found difficulty in knowing them apart. They were Charles Brassingham and his bastard brother George Ferris.

In both the resemblance to their father was very strong; Ferris, perhaps, was the more like him of the two, in that he had inherited Mr. Brassingham's brown eyes, while Charles Brassingham's were of a bright darkblue. The two young men were of the same height and build, and both possessed that intense animal vigour characteristic of the Brassingham race.

Though Ferris was altogether the darker of the two, and the expression of his face was fiercer and harder than his half-brother's, yet the short curling hair and clean-shaved faces of both added to their similarity. Each wore a heavy moustache, while in each the eyebrows were straight and darkly defined, and the chin square and massive. Neither of them was on so large a scale as Mr. Brassingham—Julian only had inherited his father's towering stature—but for symmetry and grace it would have been hard to find a pair who could match with the two young men who now stood together in Richard Ferris's courtyard.

Charles Brassingham had evidently just returned from some voyage of discovery in the neighbourhood. His face was clouded and gloomy.

"My father has returned," he said. "I have just been over to Wimbledon, and my worst fears have been confirmed. The news is all over the place that Violet is to become his wife in less than a month's time."

" There's many a slip 'twixt the cup and
the lip," replied George Ferris, in a tone of
encouragement. " It will be hard if we
cannot find some means for your meeting,
and I cannot believe Miss Champneys does
not love you, Charlie."

Young Brassingham shook his curls back
with that quick, impatient gesture Violet
had noticed when she fancied she had
identified him as the lover of another
woman. " Why should she?" said he,
hotly. "My father is rich, I have nothing;
my father has position, I am an outcast and
a vagabond ! "

" But you say Miss Champneys is not of a
calculating nature," urged Ferris. " Youth
loves youth; the young would mate with
the young. From all you have told me of
your lady-love, from the love I feel sure she
bore you until quite lately, there must be
some trickery, some lying, somewhere."

" I do not think my father is capable of a
lie in any form," answered young Brassingham ; " his faults lie all the other way,

and I cannot conceive a reason for any one else taking the trouble to make mischief between me and Violet."

" Yet mischief has been made, you yourself own," said Ferris. " Did not Miss Champneys own as much to you herself ? "

" She told me to my face she knew I loved another woman," answered Charlie, " and that it was not from what she had heard, but from what she had seen, that she knew it to be true."

" That you have given her no cause to think this since you came here I can answer for," said George ; " but was there no one at Wimbledon or in London, during the past two years, of whom she might be reasonably or unreasonably jealous ? Women in love do not want much cause to believe the worst when they fancy themselves slighted."

" I tell you. as I have told you a thousand times, George, I have not exchanged half-a-dozen words with any woman for months but Mrs. Ferris and Alice Graves ; and I

am not very likely to make love either to
your uncle's wife or your own affianced
bride."

George coloured—not with anger, but
with the happiness of undisturbed possession
—as he replied proudly, "No, I do not think
any one could have accused my Alice of
flirting with you, even if they could have
seen you together, which is impossible.
There was a time though, and not so long
ago either," continued George, rapidly, his
bronzed face crimsoning as he spoke, "when
I went as near hating you, Charlie, as I am
near loving you now."

"Hating *me*, George!" cried the other;
"and what the deuce for, may I ask?"

"Well, it is over now," said George,
"and perhaps the least said soonest mended;
but not long after you took up your quarters
here, Charlie, I overheard a conversation
between my uncle Richard and his wife
which made me mad against both you and
them."

"And you never told me, George," said

Charlie, in a vexed tone. " It was not like you to be so ' dark' with me."

" I could not tell you," answered George. " Had what Mrs. Ferris proposed been carried out there must have been war to the knife between us, however much we liked each other in old times."

Young Brassingham looked up amazed. " Go on," he said. " What was it that Mrs. Ferris proposed ? "

" My uncle's wife has always set her face against my marrying Alice Graves," replied George. " From the first moment you set foot in this house she made up her mind that she would marry you to Alice. Having no children of her own, she has centred all her hopes and ambition upon this adopted daughter, and believing, as she does believe, that your father will relent and you will be received back again into favour, she naturally preferred that Alice should be Mrs. Charles Brassingham, with both fortune and position, than that she should wed a man in my rank of life, who will have nothing but what my uncle chooses to give me."

Charles Brassingham's face flushed angrily. Had this scheming woman, thought he to himself, really dared to suppose that he, John Brassingham's only son, would mate with a girl in the position of Alice Graves? But he held his peace, and motioned George Ferris to proceed.

"It was my overhearing this project suggested by Mrs. Ferris to my uncle that made me at one time jealous of you, Charlie; for you had not then told me of your love for Miss Champneys. But when you had told me, all jealousy vanished; for I judged you by myself, and felt that your love for her was true."

There was a long pause.

Then Brassingham said suddenly, "I must see Violet again; I must have some explanation of all this misunderstanding. But who can be trusted to bring a meeting about? If you were seen at Wimbledon, people would immediately suspect my hiding-

place, and at present, at any rate, I do not
wish it known."

"You must have friends who would be
willing to serve you, whether your father
wishes you well or no," said Ferris. "Can
you not trust your sisters?"

"Anne is obstinate as a mule," replied
Brassingham; "and May is but just out of
the schoolroom. I could trust Theodora on
almost any other question but this; but she
is not over fond of Violet, and would not
lend herself to any plan for bringing about
a marriage between her and me."

"But your men-friends," urged the other.
"There must be many with whom you have
been intimate enough to trust them now.
How about this Mr. Vereker, who is going
to be your brother-in-law?"

"Pompous little prig!" was the reply.
"He would read me a lecture on truth and
justice, and recommend my quiet retirement
to the colonies."

"Why not Mr. Amory, then?"

"Pshaw! 'Cupid' Amory has his own

fish to fry. If I sent him on an errand of
that sort he would be quite certain to make
love to Violet on his own account."

"Mr. Freeman, then? From all you have
told me, he, at any rate, is trustworthy."

"Yes, I could trust Freeman just as I
could trust Theodora—in any other trouble
than the present one I really believe both
of them would do anything on earth for me
except help me to marry Violet Champneys.
I don't think they dislike her, but they
don't want her to be my wife; and even if
I knew where Freeman was, I should not
like to ask him to interfere between my
father and myself."

"Mr. Freeman is at Brassingham Park.
My uncle told me so this morning himself."

"Your uncle told you so! How on earth
does he always know every detail of what
is going on at my father's house?"

Ferris shrugged his shoulders. "How
should I know?" said he. "My uncle is a
sealed book to me. I never remember to
have been taken into his confidence ever

since he adopted me ; and, if the rumours I
sometimes hear in the neighbourhood are
true, perhaps it is just as well I should be
kept in the dark."

"How long is it since you came?" asked
young Brassingham. "It must be at least
seven years since that time we first met,
when you rescued me out of the Thames at
Mortlake. By Jove! I was very nearly
done for; but I suppose I was not born to
be drowned; reserved for a worse fate,
perhaps."

"Yes, it must be seven years ago,"
answered George Ferris. "You were a
little lad of fourteen, or so, and I must have
been just seventeen. How well I remember
that day! I was standing by the landing-
place at the Ship, just ready to start, when
I saw your canoe turn over in going through
the bridge. It was a narrow shave, Charlie!
When I dived for you the second time, I
thought there was but small chance of life,
and it was ages before we could bring you
round."

"Dear old fellow!" said Brassingham, laying his hand affectionately on the other's shoulder. "To think we should be standing here together to-day, and I your debtor still: for life then, for a home now, for love and kindness always."

The young fellow's eyes glistened as he spoke, and Ferris's somewhat stern expression softened as he heard him. The very fact of having saved Charles Brassingham's life had endeared the boy to the young man in those days, seven years ago, and now that they had both arrived at manhood, the attachment between them had lost nothing of its early romance, and had been riveted by a hundred mutual acts of friendship and the intimacy of youth's most impressionable years, when the heart is most open to the love of one's fellow men.

"It must have been some three years previous to the time you were so nearly drowned," said Ferris, presently, "that I came to live with my uncle permanently. I was then fourteen. My mother kept my

brother with her abroad, and I have never
seen either of them since. My brother was
my mother's favourite. He was much more
like her than I. He promised to be a
strapping fellow when we parted. I wonder
if we shall ever meet again?"

"Do you mean to say you have heard nothing
of them all these years?" asked Brassingham.

"Very seldom. My mother sometimes
wrote to uncle Dick on business, but I never
saw the letters; and when I asked questions
about my mother, and how my father died,
and so on, my uncle shut me up so sharp I
thought I had best let the matter drop."

"And who was your father, George?"
asked Charlie, suddenly interrupting.

"I do not know," George answered. "I
wish I did. They told me, that is, uncle
Dick and his wife, that my father was my
mother's cousin, and an awful scamp; that
he deserted my mother, and nearly broke
her heart; that he went to America, and
died there; but anything more about him I
have never been able to learn."

" Your uncle Dick was not married when
you came here first, was he, George ? "

"No; not for two years after that. His
wife was a publican's widow somewhere in
the east of London. She had a tidy income
and was better educated than uncle Dick—
had altogether more brains, in fact. She
took a fancy to his thews and sinews, and
he saw his way to independence with her
money. So they made a match of it. I
fancy the police had made it rather hot for
prize-fighters about that time, and the
' fancy ' had to look about for a means of
livelihood that could not be interfered with
by law."

" Such as marriage ! " said Brassingham,
laughing.

" Such as marriage," echoed Ferris,
gravely. "I cannot say now that I wish
my uncle had never married the woman, for
had he not, I should never have met my
Alice; but I never have liked uncle Dick's
wife, and I never shall. She has not been
actually unkind to me—uncle Dick would

never have allowed that, and she both loves
him and fears him too much to thwart him
in any way—but she is underhand and
designing; she is never happy if she has
not some scheme or plot on hand, and the
sort of fellows she gathers about this place
are questionable, to say the least of it, as
you can judge for yourself."

"I should say there was no question at
all about a good many of them," answered
Brassingham, "but those two chaps who
have been hanging about this last week are
worse by many shades than any you have
had here before. Ex-prize-fighters don't
matter; sharpers down on their luck have a
right to lodge where they please, so long as
they can pay; and, as we both know, the
house is always full of men who are keeping
out of the way for a time till their particular
horizon has cleared, but these two fellows
who are always round the corner here,
dodging about by day and by night, strike
me as a long sight blacker than the usual
class of black sheep we are favoured with.

Don't you know anything about them, George ?"

"Nothing whatever. Neither does Alice. Whatever villainy they are up to they are keeping it very dark. Here they are coming out of the house. Charlie, come into the stable, I don't want to speak to the fellows."

The two men in question had turned to speak to Mrs. Richard Ferris as they were leaving the premises, and therefore had not noticed the two young men standing in the courtyard. Mrs. Ferris's parting adjuration had evidently failed to please them. There was a lowering look on their faces as they tramped across the yard to the gate.

"I don't like the look of the job, Bill," said the slighter and better-dressed of the two men to his companion as they passed the stable where the two young men were standing in the shadow.

"Swag is swag," returned the burlier man of the two; "and I know pretty well when the swag is worth the risk; but this mixing up family rows with a big job is like to

spoil the 'boiling' and land us in the
' shop ' into the bargain. Give us a light,
Bob; I 'm fit for a ' 'bacca.' "

While a light was being obtained to the
satisfaction of the person addressed as
" Bill," snatches of conversation were
audible to Ferris and young Brassingham
in their retreat.

" Wonder what the old 'ooman wants us
for to-night, Bill. There 's more nor swag at
bottom of this 'ere lay, I reckon."

" Maybe its jist malice and devilry, Bob,
for I heard t' other old woman say, ' I 'd
stamp the life out of her afore she should
ever marry John Brassingham.' "

Then the two passed on out of the yard,
and Charles Brassingham clutched young
Ferris by the arm.

" Whom can they mean by ' she '?" he
whispered, hoarsely. " Let me go, George ";
and he struggled in Ferris's strong grasp.
" I 'll wring the truth out of their cursed
throats, if I strangle them for it ! "

" Softly, Charlie, softly," said the other,

tightening his hold on his younger companion. "Do nothing rashly, boy. To
show them they have been overheard is to
lose all chance of helping the girl, whoever
she may be."

"There has been no question of my
father marrying any other girl than Violet
Champneys," said Charlie, shaking himself
free of the other's hold. "I must at least
try to find out whither they are bound. It
is already getting dusk. I shall manage to
track them down somewhere. You go and
see if you can find out anything from Alice.
Trust me I will do nothing rashly."

George Ferris watched the youth's athletic
figure steal round the corner of the wall,
then, saying to himself, "I must not let him
go alone, lest harm should come of it," he
went swiftly into the house, and whispering
a few words to Alice to keep watch on
every one's doings in his absence, he caught
up a stout oak stick in the hall and followed
quickly in the direction Charles Brassingham
had taken.

CHAPTER V.

DICK FERRIS, THE WILLESDEN CHICKEN.

RICHARD FERRIS, *alias* Dodging Dick, *alias* the Willesden Chicken, sat smoking the pipe of rumination between the lips of doubt in the chimney-corner of his own kitchen on the evening that his nephew George and young Charles Brassingham had started off in pursuit of the men whose conversation they had overheard.

The signs of Ferris's calling were as marked on his "mug" as in the cut of his clothes and the furniture of his dwelling. He had evidently been a man of immense physical strength, as his enormous girth of chest and bull neck bore witness to.   He

was not a tall man, and his great breadth of
shoulder and muscularity of limb made him
look shorter than he really was. His complexion was swarthy, his eyes small and
deep set, and of that expressionless black
which defies the inquisition of the keenest
observer. So dark were they that they
were a perfect mask to his thoughts, except
when the gleam of anger made them lighten
with a lurid fury. But this was but once
and again in the lapse of years. Like most
men who are confident in their own strength
and powers of self-defence, Dick Ferris was
a peaceable and peace-loving man. His
fighting days had long been over; and
though the flatness of his nose gave his
clean-shaven face an unmistakable look of
the prize-fighter, yet there was something
benevolent and kindly about his smile that
attracted, and gave confidence to those who
happened to be in his society.

As he sat in his kitchen settle, with a
long clay between his thick lips, his gaitered
legs stretched out to the blaze that hissed

and crackled on the old-fashioned dogs, he looked like a respectable well-to-do yeoman, going down the hill of life certainly, but with plenty of pluck and dash in him yet, if opportunity or necessity should call upon him to discover them.

His wife's first husband had been the land-lord of a public-house in the East-End of London, where the fighting fraternity had been wont to congregate; and on his death his widow had transferred her affections and property to stalwart Richard Ferris.

Now Ferris himself was, and had always been, an honest man; that is to say, he had ever been just and honourable in his calling, was always ready to lend a helping hand to his more needy neighbours, and though a man who, from his bringing up and surroundings, was necessarily of a low moral culture, still he had his own opinions about right and wrong, and was generally supposed to have a leaning to the former.

To this predilection for the better part, the wife of Dick Ferris's bosom by no

means cordially assented, if indeed she could
be said to assent to it at all. She was a
scheming, underhand sort of woman, a liar
by nature, who found life unendurably dull
without the excitement of plot and counter-
plot for her daily stimulant. Her thorn in
the side was certainly her inability to make
Dick Ferris play Ananias to her Sapphira,
and as her husband's nephew and her own
niece, Alice Graves, failed to show any lying
proclivities, Mrs. Ferris, since her second
marriage, had had, to use her own expression,
"rather a lonesome time."

That George Ferris was the illegitimate
son of the wealthy Mr. Brassingham, of
Brassingham Park, the dame had hitherto
been completely ignorant. Not only was
Dick Ferris a man of very few words, but
secretiveness was ingrained in his nature as
thoroughly as deception was in hers. That
his sister Julia had tripped in her time
he, of course, knew full well, and that
Mr. Brassingham was the father of her two
sons he also knew; but Dick Ferris was no

schemer. He built no expectations on this left-handed connexion with the Brassingham family, any more than he felt shame that his sister should have been the mistress of the man to whom she had given her heart in years gone by. Besides, he was a man who kept his word, and he had promised his sister, before she had gone abroad, to tell no one of her connexion with John Brassingham, or that the wealthy squire was the father of her sons. With stout Dick Ferris, a promise was a promise, and the secret a secret in which the wife of his bosom had no more right to share than the stranger who bade him "good-morrow" as he passed his doors. Until, therefore, Julia Ferris, or Madame Ferrand, as she was now wont to style herself, returned to her native land, Mrs. Dick had known no more of George's birth and parentage, than did the young man himself.

Immediately, however, on Madame Ferrand's return, the old prize-fighter had been sent for by his sister, and, as a matter of course, his wife had made that sister's acquaintance.

A woman whose wits were sharpened in the school of theatrical intrigues was not long in gauging the depths of Mrs. Dick's powers of dissimulation, and in seeing that, should she ever want a friend to lend a hand to any scheme of hers, here was a woman to the manner born, who would not hesitate to plot even for plotting's sake, and who, with the additional incentive of large gain, could be moulded into a secret and devoted accomplice.

When Julia Ferrand had departed for Yorkshire, in the almost despairing hope that John Brassingham might listen to her claims, now that his wife was dead, she had not yet entrusted her sister-in-law with the secret of her life; and indeed, as long as even a glimmer of that hope remained to her, she shrank from imparting her shame to a woman who was still almost a stranger to her; but when, in that interview with John Brassingham at Bolton Abbey, the last ray of hope had been quenched in a flood of bitterness, then she had turned over in her mind the persons from whom she could get help and sympathy, and in the end she had determined to trust her brother's wife, and, if it might be, to work her own will through her assistance.

Madame Ferrand, with a view to being near to both Brassingham Park and Dick Ferris's farmhouse, had hired a small cottage at Hammersmith, which was within walking distance of both places. She had then lost no time in placing herself in communication with her brother and her brother's wife, but fearful lest George, in his devoted attachment to Charles Brassingham, should, either purposely or accidentally, mar her plans, she had not made known her presence in the neighbourhood to her son, and had strictly enjoined secrecy on both Richard Ferris and his wife.

If it were possible for the old prize-fighter's composure to be ruffled, it was so as he sat puffing at his long clay by the blaze of his bright wood fire. On that very morning his sister had announced to him her intention of placing his wife in possession of the secret of her own life and her sons' parentage, and for this purpose Mrs. Richard Ferris was now in Hammersmith. Old Ferris, who feared no man living, lived in considerable dread of his wife's tongue, and that she would not be pleased at having been kept in ignorance of the truth during their years of married life was too certain a fact to be ignored.

He had been for some time aware, as he sat smoking in his corner, that his better half had returned from her visit to his sister, for he had heard her voice giving directions to the two men who for some days had been about the premises, and had noticed the bang of her door as she had angrily slammed it on the men's departure. That she would play the part of a virago he was not at all afraid. Such was not his wife's line of business. She was too clever a woman to be a scold, too much afraid of rousing him to rage, to set no limits to the expression of her displeasure. But the calmer her manner the more certain was she to mean mischief, and Richard Ferris awaited the manifestation of her wrath with an uneasiness that was very foreign to his habitual composure.

He heard his wife's door open. Her stealthy cat-like step descended the stairs. Noiselessly she crossed the huge central hall, which Violet had described to Mr. Brassingham, where gloves, and foils, and single-sticks were hung upon the walls, or lay scattered on the floor. Silently she came up to where her husband sat, and stooping, warmed her fat white hands at the blazing fire. If she was angry there was no trace of it perceptible. Her face did not even wear that superficial smile which she was wont to use as a mask to her feelings when those feelings were bitter or vindictive.

For some moments she remained crouching before the fire, rubbing one fat hand over the other with a self-satisfied air of general contentment; then she turned slowly to her lord and master, saying, in a low pleasant voice,—

"You keep a secret well, Dick. I honour you more than I ever did before."

Dick, however, did not respond to the compliment, and his wife, still slowly smoothing the backs of her hands before the fire, became conscious that if she wanted conversation, she would have to take the larger share of it herself.

"To think that those two lads should be brothers after all," she burst out presently; "and I, living in the same house with them, never able to tell t'other from which till they opened their mouths. 'Tis a' strange world surely. Hast ever seen the other one, Dick—the one that remained with his mother? What is he like? Not a finer fellow than George or Charles, I'll be sworn."

"Never having clapped eyes on him since he was two year old, can't be supposed to know," muttered Ferris.

"Got Frenchified airs, no doubt," said

his wife. " With all his foreign training, I reckon George would open his eyes a bit, and close 'em, too, for the matter of that, in no time, if he tried on any of his dandified ways with him."

" What 's wrong with the lad, wife, that ye take up the cudgels against him already ?"

" I know nothing about him," answered his wife; " but it seems hard lines that his mother should dote upon the eldest son, and care nought about our George. Bless me! how she did run on about that Julian, how he was the handsomest and the bravest and the strongest man in the whole wide world, and the best of sons, and the truest of friends. And never a word did she ask of the other lad, who should be as dear to her as his brother."

" The other one has been always with her," said Ferris, gruffly. " She has not seen George for ten years past. How should she care? George is mine, my own adopted son; and I want no one, not even his own mother, to come between me and him."

Mrs. Ferris smelt fire. She had got on a dangerous topic, and she hastened to change the subject. In most things an easy-going man, in all things relating to his nephew Ferris was as jealous as an old maid of a young lover. He was never content when George was out of his sight, and it required even all Alice Graves's tact to prevent his being jealous of George's affection for his affianced wife. From the moment the boy had come under his care and protection, the whole heart and mind of the rough prize-fighter had undergone a wondrous change. His love for the boy had softened and mellowed his whole nature. Accustomed to use the coarsest language, he had never been known to use an oath before his nephew George. Himself a man of no particular principles, and of a very lax morality, he had striven by every means in his power to guard his young charge from even the suspicion of the evil in which his own youth had been steeped. It was therefore with a throb of pleasure rather than the reverse that he heard how little his sister seemed to regard the fate of her younger son.

"I want to understand the rights of all this history of the Brassingham diamonds," said Mrs. Ferris, presently, by way of turning her husband's thoughts from his jealous affection for his nephew. "I cannot make head or tail of the matter from what your sister has told me."

"What *has* she told you?" he asked.

"She maintains that Mr. Brassingham gave her the diamonds absolutely, and that, having been left to him as absolutely, they were his, to give to whom he pleased; that she never gave them up of her own accord; that Mr. Brassingham's father, the old man who had married the business and laid the foundations of the family prosperity, came to her house just before the birth of her second child, and after furiously insisting that, unless she forthwith left the country, she and her children should be left without a roof to

cover them or bread to eat—he carried off
the diamonds there and then. She declares
that these diamonds belong to her and to her
sons after her; that the forcible possession
taken of them by the old man was a down-
right robbery, and that, by hook or by crook,
she means to get them back into her own
possession. Now, Dick, everybody about
here knows well enough that two attempts
have been made to get hold of those
stones. What I want to know is, were you
in the job or not?"

"Maybe I was—maybe I wasn't," was the
oracular reply, as Mr. Ferris slowly emitted
a cloud of smoke from the long clay.

"Come, Dick, you may as well trust me
out and out," his wife said, coaxingly, as she
rose from her stooping position, and laid her
hand upon his knee. "I don't suppose you
are such a fool as to chum with a set of
burglars on a lay like that; but people don't
go on having a shy at the same set of jewels
time after time without being set on to do it
by those who can find the chink. It's a

dangerous game, Richard Ferris, and you know it as well as I do."

"If you mean as I know the parties who were after the diamonds, Mrs. Ferris, you may be certain sure I keeps an eye open for all them as tries to get held on 'em, and that eye wasn't shut on the gang that was the guilty parties, neither the first lay, nor the second; but if you mean that you think Dodging Dick be such a d—d fool as to risk the shop for any lot of cussed stones you could get together, why, ma'am, you're a bigger fool than I took you for."

With which not over complimentary testimonial to his opinion of his wife's acuteness, he returned to the soothing influence of his long clay.

But Mrs. Ferris was neither ruffled nor daunted by the asperity of her lawful spouse. She had been invited within the last few hours to play a part in the recapture of the diamonds which it was quite possible a British jury might consider in a far different light from that set forth by Madame Julia

Ferrand; and Mrs. Ferris had no mind to stand her trial as an accomplice in a common robbery.

"Dick, answer me this question, Do you know whether the diamonds were really your sister's property or not?"

"Yes, I do know," he answered, laying his pipe on the settle beside him, and assuming the air of a man worried into making a clean breast of it. "Yes, I do know," he repeated. "I was in the back room of my sister's apartments when that chap Brassingham gave 'em to her. He said as how they had been left him by will by some relation of his mother's; and he told Julia, there and then, and I heard him, that they were not family jewels, and that he could give them to whom he pleased. Brassingham was that spooney on Julia in those days he would have given her the moon, if he could have got it and it would have served her turn; but that was before Julian was born, and by the time George was born, he was as sick of her as ever he had been fond. The diamonds were Julia's, given her for herself, to do as she chose with —that I swear, as I am a living man—but if she takes them back again by any other way than a court of law, she'll get fifteen years over the job—that, also, I'll be sworn, or I'm not Richard Ferris."

"Then, Dick, why should she not go to law? The proof of the gift lies ready to hand with you."

"Why should she not go to law?" thundered out Ferris, starting to his feet. "What! confess herself that man's leavings before her sons? Let my George know that he is but a bastard son of a man not fit to black his children's shoes? No, never, while I live! In the old days, I never thought of shame. It did not touch me. The Ferrises were all a rough, immoral lot, and Julia was no worse than most of the girls who lived in our loose company; nor should I care a curse now what she might blab of our bad ways and goings on if it was not for the boy; but I have loved that lad, I do love him, as

if he were my own only son, and his mother
shall not blurt out the truth for the sake of
those paltry stones."

"Richard Ferris, you are raving!" sneered
his wife, with contemptuous emphasis. "Did
I not know you were a sober man, I should
say you had been at the bottle in my absence.
Do you suppose your precious nephew is so
innocent or so thin-skinned as to care one
jot who his father was so long as his parentage makes no difference to Alice Graves.
Why, man, one would think, to hear you
talk, that George had been wrapped in
cotton-wool, and brought up in a young
ladies' school. Much he'd care, indeed,
whether his father was the scamp he sup-
poses him to have been, or another, whose
chief fault would appear to be in having
given him life at all!"

"Sneer away, madam; sneer away,"
growled Ferris, as he settled himself back
in his corner, and resumed his interrupted
pipe. "'Those laugh longest who laugh
last,' and it won't be Dick Ferris who will

stand in the dock for stealing them Brassingham diamonds, nor yet will it be Dick who
will stand in the witness-box and swear to
the gift of those same diamonds by John
Brassingham to Julia Ferris five-and-twenty
years ago. So if you and she think of
wearing any of them fandangs to Court,
you'd best hit on some other ways of getting
hold of them than by highway robbery or
legal proceedings; and that's all I've got to
say about the matter!"

Mrs. Ferris was not without tact. She
saw that, in her husband's present mood, no
further information was to be extracted from
him. She rose to get supper ready, and as
she did so she thought she heard the rustle
of a dress behind the settle, but, on investi-
gation, the kitchen was empty and the door
was closed. "A mere fancy," said she, to
herself. "My talk with Julia has unstrung
my nerves." Then she laid the cloth and
spread the fare, wondering the while what
could keep the two young men so late.

CHAPTER VI.

MADAME FERRAND SEEKS ASSISTANCE.

MADAME FERRAND, as she still preferred to call herself, was ill at ease in her small home at Hammersmith. The more she pondered over the ends she had in view, the more difficult appeared the obstacles to be overcome. Should Mr. Brassingham succeed in persuading Violet to become his wife, then good-bye not only to Julian's happiness in life, but to her own obstinate hope that she might yet become her former lover's lawful wife.

Madame Ferrand really believed that Julian's devotion to Violet was in some sort returned. The doting mother, in whose eyes her son's most common-place attributes seemed superhuman in their superiority to those of other people, could not believe that a young girl of Violet's age could deliberately prefer the advances of Mr. Brassingham to the passionate worship of a splendid young fellow like her son Julian. That Charles Brassingham had tried his luck in the same quarter she had heard from her brother, Richard Ferris, and with what result she had also heard; but how that result had been brought about she did not know, nor the motives which had led her brother's wife to interfere in the love affairs of Charles Brassingham and Miss Champneys.

The return of the Brassinghams to the Wimbledon neighbourhood had not been so expeditious as was at first anticipated, and Madame Ferrand had been a fortnight at Hammersmith before she received tidings that the family had assembled at Brassingham Park for Anne's approaching marriage, and that her son Julian was a guest of Mrs. Higgins at Barnes, where the Tempests and Captain Selfe were also staying. But even then she had prepared no plan by which her object could be realized; and at last, despairing of success single-handed, she had determined to take her sister-in-law into her confidence.

Madame Ferrand's long absence from England had completely destroyed all connexion with persons of her own class in her own country; while Mrs. Ferris, on the contrary, had taken pains to improve her acquaintance in certain disreputable circles to which the callings of both her husbands had been the means of introducing her.

Dick Ferris, as a rule, was careful to remain ignorant of the reasons which induced his guests to seek a temporary asylum beneath his roof. They came and went as they would in any ordinary wayside inn, without their business being asked or their movements watched, as far as the landlord was concerned. But Mrs. Ferris had more than her share of woman's curiosity. In her first husband's lifetime she had been frequently instrumental in helping his cus-

tomers out of complicated difficulties, and, if
report were true, she had more than once
successfully assisted them to elude the pursuit of the police and get clear away to
other lands. Anyhow, it was well known in
certain circles, antagonistic to the law of the
land, that Mrs. Ferris might be trusted so
long as no suspicion of complicity was
allowed to attach to her fair fame; and in
return for such services as she might render
to offenders, not only valuables of all kinds
had found their way into her possession, but
the real lives and callings of her customers
were better known to her than to any official
at Scotland Yard.

Mrs. Ferris was, in her own way, a bit of
a philosopher. She had early turned to her
own use the Scriptural maxim concerning
the mammon of unrighteousness, and there
were at least a score of prosperous families
in the New World who would receive her,
and gladly, into their houses, were fate so
unkind as to necessitate a precipitate retirement from her own.

The two men whose conversation had been partly overheard by Charles Brassingham and George Ferris were not of the class to whom Ferris and his wife usually extended the benefit of asylum, but they had once walked in higher spheres of guilt than the one they had of late adopted, and had been known to Mrs. Ferris in the East-end of London in circumstances which made that dame think twice before refusing them admittance in their need. In short, they were better acquainted with Mrs. Ferris's own early career than that lady might wish known to the second husband of her choice. Silence for silence. There is honour amongst thieves; and the two housebreakers, for they were nothing more nor less, though as yet they remained unknown and unsuspected by the police, came and went unquestioned and unmolested at Ferris's wayside inn. Had Mrs. Ferris foreseen how futile her endeavours to foist her niece upon Charles Brassingham would prove, she might have saved herself the trouble of disturbing the

current of the latter's love-passages with
Violet ; but, at the time when her plotting brain had developed the scheme of
separating Mr. Brassingham's heir from Mr.
Brassingham's ward, she had been really
under the impression that it wanted but
time and familiarity with Alice Graves to
make young Brassingham forsake Violet for
her. In this scheme for bettering her
niece's fortunes she had been balked. She
was aware of her defeat, and had accepted
it. She had done her best for the worldly
advancement of the girl who had been to her
as a daughter. She had, according to her
lights, done her duty by her. Such a catch
as young Brassingham was not to be
manœuvred for every day ; but Alice had
preferred George Ferris, and her aunt knew
her character well enough to be aware that
she might as well try to make the Thames
flow backward as to alter Alice's mind when
once it had made its choice.

All incentive to interfere with the course
of true love between Charles and Violet being

now removed, Mrs. Ferris would willingly
have undone the mischief caused by her
anonymous letter and its results had she
known how to set about it; but she had no
intention of admitting the part she had personally played in the deception, and she did
not see her way to sending a second epistle
which should contradict the first, at any rate
while Miss Champneys was away from Brassingham Park. Scarcely had that young
lady returned before her engagement to
her guardian was made public in the neighbourhood, and entirely different views for
Miss Champneys's future disposal were ven-
tilated by Madame Ferrand with an earnestness that seemed surprising to Mrs. Ferris,
considering the girl's penniless and forlorn
position. Not till her sister-in-law had disclosed to her the whole truth of her connexion with Mr. Brassingham did Mrs. Ferris
grasp the importance of the stake for which
Madame Ferrand was playing, but, when she
had grasped it, it was with the feelings
of a keen *intriguante* that she set herself to

the checkmating of all schemes which should not accord with Madame Ferrand's and her own. She considered, and rightly, that the possession of the diamonds, even if they could be proved to be the property of Madame Ferrand, was a matter of very secondary importance to the possibility of occupying the position of Mr. Brassingham's wife ; but Mrs. Ferris was not blinded by a passionate hope, as was her sister-in-law, and her astute and matter-of-fact mind readily understood that even if Violet Champneys were removed from Madame Ferrand's path by a marriage with Madame Ferrand's son, her sister-in-law would be not one ace nearer her object of recovering Mr. Brassingham's affections or occupying the position she so coveted. Had Mr. Brassingham known and loved his illegitimate sons, and had it been possible to legitimize them, even at this late hour, by marrying their mother, there would have been some reason for such a hope on Madame Ferrand's part ; or had Mr. Brassingham been a man with whom a sense

of duty towards the woman he had seduced,
or a sense of remorse for the great wrong
done her in the past, would have weighed,
then there might have been some ground for
hope; but, according to English law, the
first case was an impossibility, and, from
what she had heard of Mr. Brassingham's
character, the second was an absurdity not
worth a thought. Believing, then, as she
did, that her sister-in-law's hopes of accom-
plishing this object were ridiculous and
futile to the last degree, Mrs. Ferris took a
practical view of the situation, and cast
about for some plan by which the diamonds,
at any rate, might be diverted into the
Ferris and Ferrand channel without endan-
gering the liberty of the persons who should
benefit by their possession. To this end she
fancied she saw her way ; and she had
hinted just so much as she chose to the two
housebreakers, not with the slightest intention of using them for the purpose of gaining
possession of the stones, but that she might
have scape-goats in reserve who might bear

the burden of suspicion, supposing her own plans should fail in any particular, when her time for action came.

The men in question had, to Mrs. Ferris's certain knowledge, been implicated in the previous attempts to obtain possession of the Brassingham diamonds, but whether in the ordinary way of housebreaking business or at the instigation of another she was not aware. Her suspicions, however, now that she knew the history of the jewels, naturally attached to her sister-in-law as the prime mover of all machinations to get hold of what she considered her own property; and, if so, the probabilities were that in sending the men to Madame Ferrand she was but re-introducing them to their old employer, with whom they could form their own plans and name their own terms without further interference on her part. In this suspicion Mrs. Ferris was partly right.

The elder and burlier of the two men whom she had sent to Hammersmith that evening, and whose name was William Cavey, had been

acquainted with Madame Ferrand when
she had first made her appearance on the
boards of a London theatre. He had but
been a " super," it is true, but the piece for
which he was engaged had a long run, and
opportunities had not been wanting for the
extraordinary beauty of the rising actress to
inflame the passions of William Cavey.

In a word, the man, like many another in
higher spheres than he, had become the
woman's slave. He had been perfectly
aware that she was Mr. Brassingham's
mistress, and that her children were Mr.
Brassingham's. He knew the story of the
diamonds. He had no doubt whatever that
as a mere matter of right the jewels belonged
to her, and he was equally sure that any
attempt to repossess herself of them by any
but legal means would only lead her into very
serious trouble, unless, perhaps, Mr. Brassingham, loth to rake up an immoral past,
should decline to prosecute. But in a man
of Mr. Brassingham's character such a
course was most improbable—not, indeed, to

be counted on for a moment—and that he would give up his claim to the stones merely from the dislike to an exposure of youthful peccadilloes was an equally absurd supposition.

When Julia Ferris had quitted England, the fascination that had held William Cavey to the theatre was gone. Such talents as he had he speedily took elsewhere, to more lucrative, if more questionable, walks in life than as a supernumerary on the London boards.

Five-and-twenty years had passed away, and the fires of William Cavey's youth burnt with a feebler glow than when he had seen Madame Ferrand last, a splendid girl of twenty, crowned with all the glow and vigour of a superb vitality. But the memory of the past still had power over the embers of his early passion; and it was with something like emotion that he again entered the presence of the woman for whom he once would have almost laid down his life.

It was thought best that one man should watch outside while the other took counsel with Madame Ferrand in her humble lodgings. Thus William Cavey went in alone.

There was nothing to fear from the police, so far as they knew, in what might be but an ordinary visit to Madame Ferrand, so Cavey bid his pal wait for him on Hammersmith Bridge, close to which Madame Ferrand's lodging was situated, and, passing through a garden fenced by a high stone wall, he was admitted to the presence of the actress who had once influenced the whole course of his existence.

She was seated by a table, on which was a lamp, which cast a mellowing light upon her still handsome features. The window-blinds were up, though the window itself was closed, and the autumn moon streamed full into the room where she was sitting. She had expected some one, a man whom her sister-in-law could trust, a man who was conversant with the ins and outs of every-

day life at Brassingham Park, who had a
cousin in the person of Miss Lavinia's maid,
and who did odd jobs about the Park, from
time to time, when trade of other sorts was
slack; but she had not expected Mr. William
Cavey.

Mr. Cavey's appearance was rough and
unprepossessing. Though he did not consider
that his calling necessitated a fur cap and the
use of fustian "extenuations,"—the dress usually assumed by the traditional outcast from
orthodox paths of industry,—yet his outward
man would not have exercised a reassuring
influence upon those whom he might meet
after nightfall. His sturdy limbs were en-
cased in the tightest of corduroys; he wore
"butcher boots" some way above the knee;
a rough blue pilot-coat was buttoned tightly
over his huge chest, and the inevitable
neckerchief of a dusky red was tied loosely
round his throat. Different, indeed, was the
Bill Cavey of present questionable life, and still
more doubtful antecedents, from the smart,
smug young actor whom Madame Ferrand

had attracted amid the turmoil of the green-
room and the flare of the footlights.

She looked up at his entrance, but no look
of recognition appeared in her dark and still
handsome eyes. The gulf of more than a
score of years, years of excitement, of
vanishing hopes, and unfulfilled desires, lay
between her and the memories of that distant
past.

She motioned him to a chair, but he took
no heed. There, before him, was the woman
whose face had made him the reckless man
he was; there she sat, a wreck indeed of the
wondrous beauty that had scorched men's
souls, but grander far, even in her ruin, than
when the noise of her early fame had placed
all the youth of the great city at her feet.
Then the beauty of a glorious animal,
radiant with health, bounding with life, had
been hers, but not the power which genius
now had stamped upon her brows—genius
and suffering combined.

The memories of the past wrestled awhile
in the breast of the burly man, whose eyes

had never been off her since he entered.
Then, with a sudden movement, he stepped
forward, and, seizing her hand, carried it
rapturously to his lips.

"Madame Ferrand! Julia Ferris! if you
have forgotten me, I have not forgotten
you," he exclaimed, as he hastily brushed
away with his sleeve what glistened in his
beady eyes. "To think that thus we should
meet again! Look at me well. Can you see
no likeness yet to any one whom you ever
know? No! Then I must tell you—I am
William Cavey!"

"Is it possible?" she exclaimed, as she
strove to maintain her composure, for his
rough gallantry had tried her already shat-
tered nerves. "Is it possible that the slim
youth I knew, with the curly yellow hair,
has changed to this! Ah! yes! I see it
now. The hair is close-cropped and iron-
grey; but the smile and the voice are the
same, and they outlast all else. I am glad
to see you, William," she continued, as she
scanned his face and figure with keen eyes—

"right glad. You were always a good friend
to me, though I had nothing to give you in
return. Friends do not grow on every
bough. But how come you here? How did
you hear of me, or know of my return to
England? I had expected a visitor to-night,
but—" and then she paused; could it be
possible that William Cavey was the man of
whom her sister-in-law had spoken? No,
surely not! She remembered William Cavey
as an *honest* man!

He hastened to explain.

"I am the person you expected," he said,
gruffly. "Are you surprised? You did not
think that the young actor, whom you remember as honest, ambitious, confident in
his own powers, could have fallen so low as
to be the companion of thieves and receivers,
the tool of any chance employer who might
want dirty work done and yet keep his own
hands clean. And you, Julia Ferris, were
the cause. I do not reproach you; you need
not reproach yourself. It was not your
fault; you could not help a man's passions

being roused by your beauty, or his head being turned by your cleverness. Bah! it is an old story! What need to tell it to you now? I was no more to you than the dirt beneath your feet, while day after day I endured the sight of rich, young, handsome Brassingham basking in the love I longed for. I knew how it must be in the end, but I did not think he would have tired so soon. I was given a good engagement in the provinces just at the time your second boy was born; I took it, hoping that the day might come when, left by him, you would perhaps turn to me. Then I heard he had left you, and I hurried back to town. I had thrown up my engagement only to find you flown. Then I took to drink. Need I say more? I went from bad to worse—honour, honesty, ambition, hope, were all quenched one by one; then, when friendless and penniless, I fell in with the set who used to meet at Sam Graves's public: I cast in my lot with theirs, and became the man you see here to-night."

" And am I any better, or better off ? " she
exclaimed, half angrily, half pitifully.
" Have my sins been so lightly punished
that you must upbraid me with your own
ruin ? "

" I do not upbraid you," he replied. " The
reason I remind you of the past is that I
may account to you for my knowledge of
the business for which you sent for me here
to-night. You had told me of your diamonds ; you had shown them me. Do you
not remember that when you feared to wear
the stones because of their great value, it
was to me you entrusted the jewels to have
their counterpart made in paste ? I brought
you back both sets. John Brassingham's
father robbed you of the real ones—you
deemed the others worthless. I asked you
for them and you gave them me. I have
them still. Twice have I tried to get the
real stones, and twice I have been foiled ;
but no suspicion has attached to me as yet.
I am poor, I am degraded, I am reckless,
but my love for you will never die. I do

not expect, I do not hope, that you will ever care for me; but for your sake I will risk another trial, and, if I win, the stones are yours. A share you shall give me, enough to prosper with in some colony. I cannot work alone, and my pal, who is now waiting on the bridge, must have his share. Are you agreed?"

Madame Ferrand had bowed her head upon her hands. She was violently agitated; her frame trembled with excitement. She had invited her sister-in-law to send her some one to whom she might safely disclose her own little plots and plans, and here was a master-mind who took the whole matter out of her feeble hands at the very outset,— a man whose education had fitted him for better things fallen to the condition of a common thief! Was she to set on the man who loved her to rob the man she loved? That was the question she was called upon to answer. Could it cure her pain or heal her heart-ache, if all the diamonds in the world were hers? And, if the stones were

traced to her, would not John Brassingham's
heart be more utterly closed to her even
than before? But if she left him in undisturbed possession, whose would the jewels
be,—his wife's? Yes, of course, his wife's!
A vision of Violet, young, fair, and innocent, crowned with the glittering gems that
had once been given HER by John Brassingham's own hands, rose before her eyes;
Violet, whom at one moment she loathed
with a hatred unutterable, because John
Brassingham loved her, and whom at the
next she yearned towards with a mother's feelings, because the girl was the beloved of her
own darling son. No! as Mrs. Brassingham,
Violet should never wear those jewels.
Should Julian's suit prevail, then at some
future day the gems should pass into the
hands of Julian's wife!

"I am agreed," she said, suddenly looking
up, and taking Cavey's horny hand in hers.
"Get me the jewels, and I will pay you what
you like."

As she spoke, and as she held his hand in

solemn pledge of their covenant, a slight
rustle was heard among the shrubs, the
boughs of the mountain-ash that over-
shadowed the windows waved violently to
and fro, a fall as of heavy bodies was heard
on the outside of the wall, and the next
moment a figure came swiftly up the garden,
which, by the light of the moon, Cavey recognized as that of his pal, Bob Lane.

Instantly divining danger of some sort or
another, Cavey rushed to the door. The
moonlight streamed full upon him and
Madame Ferrand by his side, as Lane joined
them in the porch.

Lane was breathless with running.

" You are being watched," he gasped;
" there, from those trees "; and he pointed to
the clump of mountain-ash, whose scarlet
berries clustered about the very windows of
the cottage. " I saw the trees shake
strangely," he continued, " as I stood upon
the bridge. I watched the place, but the
moon became over-clouded, and all was
dark. Then, when the clouds had passed,

I saw two men climb up the wall and hide among the boughs. I rushed across to warn you, but they were gone. They must have seen me as I crossed the road."

Quick as lightning, Cavey sprang among the trees and swung himself up to the top of the wall, but not a soul was to be seen. Then he bade Lane and Madame Ferrand enter the room in which conversation had been carried on, and talk in a high-pitched key; but not even when he stood close to the window could the words of the speakers be distinguished. Satisfied that, whatever might have been seen, nothing could have been overheard, Cavey re-entered the house. Having dismissed Lane to the garden-gate, he hastened to reassure Madame Ferrand's nervous fears. Nothing further could be settled on that night. He would sleep upon his plans, he said, and communicate to her on the morrow some definite line of action. Then he took his leave, and the two tramped back again along the road by which they had come, and returned by midnight to Ferris's quaint old inn.

CHAPTER VII.

GEORGE FERRIS RECOGNIZES HIS MOTHER.

FAVOURED by the dusk of evening, Charles Brassingham and George Ferris had been enabled to follow Cavey and Lane into Hammersmith without being themselves observed.

They had witnessed the parting of the two men at the end of Hammersmith Bridge, and had seen Cavey enter the garden of a house not far from the bank of the river.

The tops of the mountain-ash trees were visible above the wall, and immediately suggested a safe ambush, if the wall itself proved surmountable.

Taking advantage of a moment when

dark clouds obscured the moon, young Brassingham had mounted upon Ferris's shoulders, and then, sitting astride the wall, had
hoisted his companion into position by his
side. The clump of ash-trees grew on a rising
mound, which diminished the height of
masonry upon the inner side, and rendered
escape an easy matter in case their presence
should be discovered.

But though by the moonlight, as well as
by the soft glow of the lamp, they were both
able to witness the interview between
Madame Ferrand and Cavey, yet not a
sound had reached them of the conversation.

At first, from their position among the
trees, the two young men had only been
able to distinguish the sturdy figure of
Cavey, in butcher boots and pilot coat,
standing alone just within the door; then,
when he moved across the room, the young
men had pressed further forward, and had
seen him stoop over a woman's hand and
lean towards her in the attitude of one who

was offering a caress. But as the woman
had risen hurriedly from her seat, they had
started back further into the clump of trees,
and had remained for some minutes in doubt
whether their presence had been discovered.

" There is nothing to be gained by staying here," whispered Ferris to Brassingham.
" I don't believe this visit has anything to
do with what we overheard, and we have
had a two mile tramp on a fool's errand."

" We at least know where to get information, or, if we can't get it ourselves, we can
put the police on the track, if any harm
should happen to Violet," returned the
other.

" Ay, lock the door when the steed is
stolen. Much use that will be," said Ferris,
whose temper was none the better for being
dragged into Hammersmith at this hour, on
what he considered a wild goose chase.

" Hush! Keep back!" said Brassingham,
pulling Ferris further into the shadow of the
trees. " They are coming close to the
window."

As he spoke, Madame Ferrand had raised her head from her hands, and had wearily crossed the room, and gazed out over the river, while the moonlight fell full upon her worn, but still beautiful face.

A low, smothered cry broke from George Ferris, as the face, white and sad and troubled, rested for a moment against the window-pane. With a sudden movement that nearly sent Charles Brassingham crashing among the boughs, Ferris clutched his companion by the arm, and pointed to the woman's figure as she stood out clear and defined in the streaming moonlight.

"My mother! It is my mother!" he exclaimed in a voice husky with emotion. "How comes she here? To think that I should be playing the spy on her! Who is this man that he should dare? Heavens! what can it mean?"

He retreated towards the top of the mound, on which the mountain-ash trees grew, while Brassingham, amazed, grasped the slender trees, as he quickly followed him.

The commotion caused by their hurried scramble through the boughs had caught the watchful eyes of Lane, as he stood upon the bridge, and had been heard even by Cavey and Madame Ferrand within the house. Quickly, but heavily, they had dropped from the wall into the lane below, and their fall had been heard by the occupants of the sitting-room, and by Lane as he sped across the road that ran by the river's bank. But they had a clear start. By the time the alarm was given, and Cavey had rushed amongst the trees, they had mingled with the throng of people in Hammersmith, and were safe from all probable recognition or pursuit.

Accustomed as Charles Brassingham was to witnessing furious outbursts of feeling and passion in George Ferris, he was rather taken aback by the almost frenzied condition of excitement produced in him by this unexpected recognition of his mother.

That she should be in England, in Hammersmith, close to *him*, her own son, leaving him in ignorance of her presence, was in itself cause for keen sorrow to a nature so affectionate as that of George Ferris. As might be expected in a man who embodied the characteristics of two such families as the Brassinghams and the Ferrises, all animal instincts were developed to their highest pitch in him. If in some respects his passions were those of the savage, his affections were those of the savage also. Educated he was not, clever he was not, nor had he acquired that crown of civilized virtues—self-control; but in his love for woman, in his chivalrous friendship for Charles Brassingham, and in devotion to those who had been his guardians and benefactors, all the strong, rough goodness of his nature came bright and unsullied from his generous heart within. Of all his unreasoning instincts his love for his mother was the strongest. In him it *was* an instinct; for the ties of gratitude, the memories of a guiding touch and a soft caress, had but little to do with the feeling of devotion with which he regarded the only parent he had ever known. But what most pervaded the current of young Ferris's thoughts was the mysterious connexion between his mother and Cavey. What connexion could there be that should warrant a visit to her alone late at night—a conference sealed by a caress? Though, by long acceptance of the lie, young Ferris had at last brought himself to suppose that his mother's husband had been her cousin, and that, according to the story palmed upon him in childhood, his father had really died in some foreign land, yet finding no relations on his father's side, and looking to Dick Ferris's ominous silence whenever he was questioned on this theme, it could not be but that the young man had made shrewd guesses of his own as to the real, unhappy truth. That immediately on his mother's secret return to England Cavey should have access to her, when even her own son. was kept in ignorance of her arrival; that this man should be, as he evidently was, on terms of privileged, even familiar, intimacy, could not but breed in George Ferris's mind a horrible suspicion that he might find, in this broken-down reprobate—whose reputation was even too questionable for Dick Ferris's most questionable connexion—the father whom he had never known, the husband of the mother he so loved. If this should prove to be the case, how was his pride humbled, to own for father a man who, at any rate among the set who frequented his uncle's bar, had the character of a drunkard, a receiver, and a thief!

Moody and sullen, with fitful bursts of rage and mortification, Ferris strode back to his uncle's house. He could not bring him-self to suggest, even to Charles Brassingham, the hideous supposition that had taken possession of his mind. Only one thing was certain—that until the relation between Cavey and his mother was satisfactorily cleared up no steps could be taken which might set the police upon the track of Cavey's delinquencies, if a hundred Violets had to suffer in consequence of the delay. An interview with his uncle he must have; but when he arrived at home his uncle had retired for the night, and to Mrs. Ferris it was quite impossible that he should confess his evening's adventure.

Neither was William Cavey in a communicative mood, as he and his pal tramped back to Ferris's. That George Ferris was the nephew of the ex-prizefighter, Cavey was, of course, aware; but that he was the son of his old love by John Brassingham had not occurred to him. Besides, Cavey was not of the set who habitually made use of Ferris's as an asylum in times of trouble, his mode of life being too questionable even for Mr. Richard Ferris to put up with; consequently it had only been within the last few days that he had been brought in contact with either the legitimate or illegitimate sons of his rival. The extraordinary resemblance between the two young men had, of course, struck him, as it struck all who saw them together; but his time was too fully occupied with his own

pressing needs for him to waste it in profit-
less speculations on what, after all, might be
but a chance resemblance.

Now, however, that he knew the truth, it
did seem strange that fate should have
drawn together, in the bonds of a firm
friendship, these two young half-brothers,
each ignorant of their relationship throughout the many years of their affectionate intercourse, and that Charles Brassingham, cut off
from his own family, should have found shel-
ter and a home beneath the same roof as the
son of the woman who might have stood
in his own mother's place.

The business in hand demanded prompt
action, however. Means must be found by
which the internal economy of Brassingham
Park should be known to the conspirators.
The whereabouts of the diamonds must be
found out, and the best opportunity discovered for gaining possession of them.
Such aid as could be expected from Miss
Lavinia's maid was not sufficient. It seemed
obvious that some one bound up in the plot,

skilled in deception, capable of assuming a
part at will, should be selected to obtain
admission, if possible, into Mr. Brassingham's house ; who, while mixing freely with
the inmates, both above and below stairs,
should be able to gain the information required, and forward the designs of those who
could not obtain admittance. Such a person
seemed to be found in Madame Ferrand
herself.

CHAPTER VIII.

MR. WILLIAM CAVEY LAYS A TRAIN.

THE following morning Cavey, acting upon his last inspiration, donned a suit of seedy black, such as might be suitable for the character of a Scripture reader in indigent circumstances, and arming himself with a well-thumbed volume of hymns and a dilapidated cotton umbrella, proceeded on a visit to his cousin Jane Cavey, Miss Lavinia Brassingham's maid, at Brassingham Park. The picture of snug respectability, he presented himself at the door of the servants' hall and obtained admittance. He informed Miss Cavey that he was very anxious to find a situation, even temporarily, for a friend of

his in almost destitute circumstances, who
could produce the best of characters, was an
excellent workwoman, a professed dressmaker—in short, a person who would prove
a perfect jewel to her employers. Did his
sweet cousin Jane know of a family in want
of such a person ?

Yes; his sweet cousin Jane did know of
such a family, and that family was no other
than the Brassinghams themselves. The
dressmaker who had undertaken the wedding
order for the bridesmaids' dresses was down
with fever. The young ladies were at their
wits' end to get their costumes ready in time;
and much of Miss Anne Brassingham's
trousseau had been left unmade from the
lack of hands to do the work. If the young
person Mr. Cavey spoke of could make it convenient to step up to Brassingham Park the
very next day, Miss Cavey believed it would
take quite a load off the Misses Brassingham's minds; and, delighted at the chance
which had sent a good dressmaker to lighten
her own labours at this critical juncture,-

Miss Cavey tripped off to tell her news, and
to ask permission for the young person to
come to the house, where she could work
under the superintendence of the young
ladies themselves.

Naturally the proffered assistance was
eagerly accepted. Miss Cavey conveyed the
gracious permission to her worthy but indigent relative, and was told that Mrs.
Steele, the dressmaker in question, should
arrive at Brassingham Park on the following
day. After a few more runs up and down
stairs, and confabulations between mistresses
and maid, it was decided that Mrs. Steele's
services were too urgently required to admit
of the waste of time involved in a daily
journey to and fro between London and
Brassingham Park, and that if Mrs. Steele
could kindly make it convenient, it would
be as well for her to remain entirely at the
Park until the approaching wedding was
celebrated.

In high feather at his unlooked-for success, Mr. William Cavey retraced his steps

as far as Hammersmith, where, hymn-book in hand, and the cotton umbrella beneath his arm, he called for the second time on Madame Julia Ferrand.

So complete was the change in his appearance, that not even so practised an eye as Madame Ferrand's in the matter of disguises recognized the burly "rough," whose appearance had so startled her the night before.

In place of fustian pants, so tight as to show every muscle of his limbs, thrust into boots that suggested the highwayman of old, Cavey had donned a pair of threadbare "extenuations" that flopped about his nether limbs like two black pillow-cases tied together at their necks. The costermonger's neckerchief was replaced by a limp collar and a soiled white tie; the pilot jacket by a long frock coat; the peaked cap by a high hat, much worn as to its nap, much crushed as to its crown. Even the sturdy, defiant manner of the man had altered to a cringing air of deprecation, which seemed as natural a part of his new character as bullying swagger had of his old one.

He soon unfolded to Madame Ferrand the plan he had in his mind. Accustomed as she was to assume all manner of parts, being not only an accomplished actress, but a milliner and dressmaker by profession before she had trodden the stage, she was in all ways admirably fitted to fill the situation so opportunely offered to her.

Not only would she now be able to discover where the diamonds were kept, but she would hear whether they would be worn at the approaching nuptials, and by whom; whether Anne Brassingham, who claimed them through her mother's will, would wear them as her bridal ornaments, or whether they were reserved to adorn the person of John Brassingham's second wife.

Nor was this all. By accepting the post Cavey had procured for her, she would be on the spot to espouse her son's cause with Violet Champneys, and to poison her mind

against her other suitors. If there was *any*
way in which Violet's marriage with Mr.
Brassingham could be obstructed, surely a
scheming jealous woman, lodged in the same
house with the persons whose union she
desired to hinder, would be able to find it
out and act upon it. Here was an unexpected road into the enemy's very cita-
del. No one there but Mr. Brassingham
himself had ever seen Madame Ferrand
before. She was a perfect stranger to all
others at the Park. That Julian would be
about the house was likely, but even if
he should recognize his mother in her
disguise, which was improbable, he had
been forewarned not to disclose his recog
nition.

Cavey expressed his intention of taking
up his quarters at Ferris's, until Anne Brassingham should have become Mrs. Vereker,
so as to be close at hand in any emergency,
and he added that the counterfeit diamonds
would be ready to hand whenever opportunity occurred for an exchange.

Madame Ferrand entirely concurred in
William Cavey's views.   The excitement
of the adventure was agreeable to her, the
risk small, the incentive and the reward
alike great.   She declared herself prepared
to carry out the part assigned her.   She
would be ready to accompany him to Brassingham Park on the following day, and she
would venture to say that her disguise should
be so complete that even he should not know
her for Madame Ferrand.

Matters having been thus satisfactorily set
in train, Cavey took his departure; and
Madame Ferrand, leaning her head against
the window-pane, as was her habit when in
deep thought, fell into a reverie on the
strangeness of the part she was now called
upon to play—a spy in the house of the
father of her sons, the lover of her early
youth, in the house she had never yet
entered, though the days had been when she
had aspired to be its mistress, and to which
a despairing hope still impelled her, in the
idea that, by her strength of will and mar-

vellous powers of intrigue, she might yet
secure Violet's love for her darling son,
and perhaps fill the blank in John Brassingham's life that the loss of Violet would
cause.

CHAPTER IX.

MADAME FERRAND TAKES SERVICE AT BRASSINGHAM.

WHILE Cavey had been absent on his visit to Brassingham Park, George Ferris had taken his uncle aside, and had informed him of his last night's adventure from beginning to end. He had expressed to him his doubts whether the presence of such men as Cavey and Lane upon the premises was not likely to get the inn "blown upon" to the police. He had implored him to prevent any harmful plot against Miss Champneys's happiness being hatched by such men as he believed Cavey and Lane to be, and after having spoken with much bitterness of his mother's arrival in Hammersmith, while he, her own

son, was kept ignorant of the fact, he had
pressed his uncle for information as to the
connexion existing between his mother and
Cavey, and the meaning of the latter's noc-
turnal visit to Madame Ferrand, which, to
his mind, appeared mysterious.

The elder Ferris was not disposed, however, to afford the younger any information
on the subject; nor, indeed, did he himself
hold the key to many of his nephew's questions. That his wife had reasons for believing
that Cavey and Lane could be useful to his
sister, and had on that account not only
brought them to the inn, but had told them
where Madame Ferrand could be found, he
was, of course, perfectly well aware; but of
any previous acquaintance existing between
his sister and Cavey he was as ignorant as
George himself, nor could he throw any light
upon the apparent understanding now existing between them.

Instead of sympathizing with his nephew's
anxieties on behalf of the young lady on
whom young Brassingham had set his affec-

tions, Dick Ferris was rather inclined to rebuke him for meddling with other people's business, and to be angry that he allowed himself to play the spy, even when the conversation that had been overheard appeared to justify such a proceeding.

He pointed out to his nephew that, whatever the "job" spoken of by Cavey and Lane might be, the expressions they had made use of pointed rather to some attempt to interfere with Miss Champneys's marriage with the elder Brassingham, and had nothing to do with her personal comfort or safety, or with her past relations with Charles Brassingham. That if, indeed, there should be any plot on foot for preventing Mr. John Brassingham's second marriage—and even of this Dick Ferris professed himself ignorant —the scheme would be favourable to Charles Brassingham's hopes, and had best not be interfered with by that young gentleman himself. Finally, Dick Ferris expressed his opinion that the snatches of conversation overheard by his nephew had nothing to do with

Cavey's visit to Madame Ferrand, and that
George had better wait to speak to his
mother until she should send for him, which
she would probably do before many days
were over.

With this explanation—if explanation it
could be called—George Ferris had to be
content. It was impossible to confess to his
mother how he had become acquainted with
her place of residence. It was equally
impossible to tax Cavey with criminal intentions of any sort, now that he knew of his
familiar intimacy with his mother, and more
especially now that he was haunted by the
suspicion that this man might turn out
to be his own father. That he, of all persons, should be the first and only man
admitted to his mother's cottage seemed to
point to such a probability; that he should
have been apprised of her return to England
even before her own son was made aware of
it, served to strengthen the unwelcome conviction. In age and appearance there was
nothing to render the fact of his standing in

such a relation to Julian and George impossible or even improbable ; and, moreover, it was evident that some mysterious reasons had hitherto existed why the thread of connexion between the Ferris family and Cavey should never be entirely snapped.

All these considerations helped to paralyze George Ferris's will in taking steps to defeat any plans Cavey might be engaged in carrying out. What George thought or wished, Charles Brassingham usually thought and wished too. So Mr. Cavey was freed from a surveillance which, under other circumstances, he could not but have found embarrassing, and perhaps obstructive, to his designs.

Meanwhile Mrs. Ferris, informed by Cavey of the daring plot to place Madame Ferrand within the very house of Mr. Brassingham, hurried off to her sister-in-law's cottage in Hammersmith to give what assistance she could in the transformation of her outward appearance.

She was too late, however, to be of any

use. The stooping grey-haired woman who blinked at her from behind her glasses as she opened the door, admitted her to Madame Ferrand's apartment, kept her in conversation for some moments, in the belief that she was talking to the landlady of the house, and then, dropping her disguises of dress, manner, and gait, laughed at her for being so easily taken in. Her disguise was certainly complete. A large cap of muslin, stiff and white, covered not only the grey wig that concealed her own dark hair, but much of her forehead as well, thus considerably altering the shape of the face. The spectacles changed not only the colour but the expression of her eyes; a ruff of stiff white muslin enveloped her throat and neck. Her black dress, entirely without ornament or trimming, was relieved only by a steel châtelaine, to which were attached scissors, keys, and other items that proclaimed her the dressmaker and housekeeper she professed herself to be.

Neither Mr. Brassingham nor Julian Fer-

rand, should she happen to meet either,
would penetrate this disguise.

Dick Ferris had not thought fit to impart
to his wife the adventures of his nephew
and Charles Brassingham. Madame Ferrand, therefore, was still in ignorance that
her presence in England was known to her
younger son.

The story of Charles Brassingham's attachment to Miss Champneys was, however, duly
impressed upon her by her sister-in-law, as
well as the deception which had been practised upon the latter through the uncon-
scious agency of her own son George. Mrs.
Ferris dwelt much on the extraordinary
likeness between the two young men as well
as upon their romantic attachment to one
another. Lastly, she conjured Madame Ferrand, if she had set her heart upon wedding
Violet to Julian, to widen the breach between
that young lady and Charles Brassingham
by every means in her power. " For," said
she, " the girl's distress was far too genuine,
when she was convinced of his defection, to

make it safe to give her the slightest chance
of being undeceived. Your only chance of
marrying her to your son is by proving to
her the falsehood of her own love, Charles
Brassingham, and the evil of his father's
early career. Make her believe that her
own marriage to the elder Brassingham
must necessarily work your own failure and
ruin, and she will fly from that marriage
as she fled from marriage with the son. It
will be your own fault if, in her bewilderment
and desolation, you cannot convince her of
your own son's devotion, and wed her to
him without more ado."

All which advice Madame Ferrand promised to mark, learn, and inwardly digest.

The arrival of Mr. Cavey in his threadbare go-to-meeting suit, to escort Madame
Ferrand to her new situation, put an end to
the conversation between the two women.
Mrs. Ferris was to see to the disposal of
Madame Ferrand's goods and chattels at a
neighbouring warehouse. The landlady was
settled with, and informed that Madame

Ferrand was about to return to the Continent. The cab containing Mrs. Steele, as she was now to be called, and Mr. William Cavey, was driven to the station at Charing Cross, to give colour to their parting statement. From thence the pair were not long in making their way to their real destination—Brassingham Park.

CHAPTER X.

THE VEREKER FAMILY.

ON the return of the Brassinghams to their home near Wimbledon, the arrangements for Anne's wedding had gone on apace. Invitations had been issued not only to the church and breakfast, but a grand fancy ball was to be given at Brassingham Park on the evening of the wedding-day.

It wanted now but a week to the date fixed for the marriage. The house was full of guests. Vere Vereker's bachelor uncle and two maiden aunts had arrived, and were to remain over the fancy ball, to the very great discomfiture of all the younger portion of the guests; for the bachelor uncle was a valetudinarian, and as full of fads as an egg

is of meat, while the maiden aunts objected
to almost every amusement, on the ground
of its being frivolous or ungodly.

They were ladies of the extremest evan-
gelical views, utterly committed to the fatal
error that their own mission in life was, or
ought to be, to disseminate Calvinistic doc-
trines, and to withstand the world, the flesh,
and the devil with boldness, wherever they
considered they had discovered them. In
so worldly a family as the Brassinghams,
these ladies were sure to get peeps at the
cloven hoof every hour of the day. Had
they maintained silence they believed that
they would have but shirked their duty; nor
were they of opinion that they could meet
the evil by retreating from Brassingham
Park; for did they not owe a sacred duty to
the son of their departed brother in standing
by him in this most important crisis of his
life ?

Among themselves, Mr. Nathaniel Vereker
and his sisters Elizabeth and Caroline greatly
deprecated their nephew's choice of a wife.

Their zeal for propagating what they called the true gospel had not abated their family pride, and it was a grievous shock to them that a Vereker should take to wife the daughter of a mere mushroom like John Brassingham. The Verekers, when they had married at all—which in the last two generations had not been often—had always chosen from among their own class, which, it is needless to say, was, in their own estimation, the first in the land. Now the Brassinghams did not belong to that class. Their wealth had failed to gain them admission to the society of the county families. They were not vulgar, because they had no affectation, but still they were *parvenus*.

But there were other reasons why the Vereker kindred disliked their nephew's choice. Anne Brassingham was an obstinate and, at times, a violent, woman. She would not have been a true Brassingham without these characteristics. Now Vere was not violent, but he was as obstinate as, or

more so than, his bride elect; and, if ever the
season of matrimonial storms set in, there
seemed to be less chance of mutual forbearance than is generally hoped for in such
circumstances.

Vere was the only son of an elder brother
of the trio of Verekers who had come to
Brassingham Park to be present at their
nephew's wedding; but Vere's father had
not been the head of the Vereker family.
A first cousin of his father's, Lord Vassalis,
held the title and estates of the Vereker family,
and Vere had nothing but the disadvantage
of being nearly connected with the " Upper
Ten " without any adequate means of keeping
up his position. Vere's father had made an
improvident marriage in his own rank. The
lady had been a granddaughter of a poor
Scotch peer, with very little but her high birth
to recommend her. She had been proud
and full of prejudices of caste and nation,
penurious to meanness, and of a quarrelsome
disposition. So Vere's inherited characteristics were hardly such as were calculated to

make him an indulgent husband or a generous man.

The Misses Vereker, Elizabeth and Caroline (never had the Christian names of these
Roman-nosed spinsters been suffered to dege-
nerate into abbreviations), had come next in
order of birth to Vere's father; but Nathaniel
was the Benjamin of the family, and, though
some ten years older than his nephew Vere,
had always been the "baby" brother of his
two maiden sisters. From having nothing
to occupy his time, and just enough money
to be enabled to avoid the necessity of
working for his living, Nathaniel Vercker had
gradually developed, in his own estimation,
every imaginable physical ill that flesh is
heir to. A new symptom was a godsend to
him. If it did not appear when he considered it ought to have appeared, his
nervous fancies invented it, and he would
straightway treat himself for his new com-
plaint with an assiduity and attention worthy
of a better cause.

"Poor dear Nathaniel's" delicate health

was of course a constant source of anxiety to
his spinster sisters; but to a family like the
Brassinghams, whose rude vigour of nerves
and constitution never admitted fanciful
ills into their daily life for a moment, " poor
dear Nathaniel " was an unmitigated bore.

Theodora, always a bad hand at suppress-
ing any feeling of disgust or contempt for
human weaknesses, was sufficiently unsuccessful in the present instance as to rouse the
protective instincts of the Misses Vereker to
their fiercest height. The two old ladies
had never before had to draw upon their
Christian forbearance to so large an extent
in abstaining from the strongest expressions
in their vocabulary towards Anne's handsome
sister; but they made up for immediate
restraint by a daily register of their debts to
Theodora, which was destined to be paid in
other days with interest.

CHAPTER XI.

EXPLAINS THE POSITION OF AFFAIRS AT BRASSINGHAM.

In the midst of all the hurry and bustle of the preparations for the wedding, Anne alone was careless and lethargic. One would have supposed from her manner that she was the person least concerned in the ceremony which was to be the climax of all this confusion.

Whatever love-making went on in the house, it was certainly not between the bride and bridegroom elect. On matters of business they sometimes held council, now with Mr. Brassingham, now with the family solicitor, now with the upholsterer who was to furnish their house in town ; but they quite understood each other that they would

probably see a good deal of one another
before "death did them part," and they
were of one mind to postpone all blandish-
ments to some remote period of their future
lives.

The more Mr. Brassingham forced his
attentions on unhappy little Violet, the more
the girl shrank from him. Daily his passion
for her increased, as the time when he might
claim her for his own drew near, and daily
she drooped like some shade-loving flower
scorched and withered by the sun's fierce
rays. Never could she raise her head without meeting his bold brown eyes fixed on
her with a passionate yearning; never could
she stroll out into the open air without finding his colossal figure close at her side. Had
she loved him, how proud would she have
been of her supremacy; how joyful in the
sense of power over this splendid specimen
of manhood; how glad in his strong protection; how restful in the warm tenderness of
his great love! But it was the old, old story:
"*L'un qui baisait, l'autre qui tendait la joue*";

his love and his passion were squandered in vain, and their very strength and persistency only served to increase her aversion.

As it was, Violet's nerves began to give way under the constant strain. To love one man and to be engaged to marry another proved less possible than she had imagined. The accusing image of her lost love dwelt with her by day and haunted her in her feverish dreams. The more her imagination dwelt upon the son, the greater the aversion she discovered to the father.

Julian Ferrand, who had for some time past been the guest of the Higginses, was, with one or another of the Higgins household, constantly at Brassingham Park. Indeed, Mr. Brassingham, ignorant of his influence over Violet, and caring much more for Julian's society than he did for that of any other of the young men who were usually about the place, encouraged his visits by every courtesy in his power, and pressed daily hospitalities upon him.

But the influence of Julian Ferrand over

Violet had undergone a subtle change since
his electric power had produced such an
extraordinary effect upon her by the Yorkshire stream.

In the first place, Ferrand, though rough
and unpolished, was at heart an honourable
man. Though his love for Violet Champneys
was undiminished, her engagement to Mr.
Brassingham was to him an insurmountable
obstacle to the prosecution of his own suit;
the more so as, except by accepting Mr.
Brassingham's hospitality, he could not have
gained access to Violet's society.

Again, he had become aware, through
Frank Freeman and Agatha Bonchurch,
with both of whom he had become exceed-
ingly intimate since his arrival in the Wimbledon neighbourhood, of the love passages
which had once existed between Miss Champneys and Mr. Brassingham's son Charles,
whom as yet he had never seen. The story,
as told by them (and even they did not know
how deeply Violet's heart had been touched),
had explained to Julian Ferrand much that

had hitherto been inexplicable to him in Miss Champneys's conduct. He saw now that she had been drawn to him not by love nor by coquettishness, but because his society was a relief from the persistent love-making of the elder Brassingham ; and that she should be compelled by circumstances of which he was ignorant to give her hand to the father while her heart was with the son, filled him with a pity as great even as his love. Not only was Ferrand's nature greatly changed by his love itself, but his surroundings and associations, ever since he had first gone to the Yorkshire Wells, had considerably influenced his rugged nature, and at each contact had broken away some of the rough surface, and had discovered glimpses of the brilliancy of that which was beneath.

Freeman's inexplicable liking for him had increased tenfold since their first meeting at the " Wells," and had become an enthusiasm, with which, in a modified degree, he had succeeded in inspiring Miss Bonchurch as well. Minds of so high a type, so justly balanced, and so self-controlled, were something quite without the bounds of Julian Ferrand's past experiences. That he should be an object of friendly interest to them first surprised and then flattered him. He freely admitted their influences; he had the natural intelligence to profit quickly and largely by their conversation. The elevated mental atmosphere in which they both lived gradually affected his whole being, and transformed the merely animal proclivities of his nature into the refined gold of a lofty humanity.

Any intention of friendly interference with Miss Champneys's choice by Frank Freeman had necessarily been abandoned when her engagement to the elder Brassingham had become an accomplished fact. Mr. Monckton's information had only been acquired at second-hand; and the locality lying between Hammersmith, Acton, and Isleworth was rather a large one in which to search for Dick Ferris's tavern, where it was

supposed that Charles Brassingham had
found a home. During the first week of
Freeman's visit to Brassingham Park he
had explored every old haunt of Charles
Brassingham's, in the hope of getting from
his own lips the story of his attachment and
its disappointment. But neither in London
nor in Wimbledon, neither in Putney,
Barnes, nor Mortlake, could he gain any
tidings of his old friend. He had visited
the wayside inn, where the Rev. Silas
Monckton had been so unceremoniously
treated by George Ferris; but the woman
who had then been dying was now dead, the
business had changed hands, and the bar-
maid, who might at least have thrown some
light upon the identity of Charles Brassingham's companion, had disappeared into the
whirlpool of London pot-houses, and had left
no trace behind her.

Mindful of his promise to his mother before
the " Wells " party had left Yorkshire,
"Cupid" Amory, on his return to Wimbledon, had adopted a tone of Platonic friendli-

ness with Theodora and May which, while it
deceived neither of them, only made it more
uncertain than ever whether he meant to
propose to the one, the other, or neither.
That the matter should not die a natural
death Miss Anne Brassingham took good
care. Though she was not particularly concerned about the ultimate settlement in life
of either of her sisters, yet, as the eldest, and
as mistress of her father's house until her
marriage, she liked to exercise her preroga-
tive while she could, even in the settlement
of her sisters' love-affairs, so far as she was
able to interfere. Though she was by no
means certain which it was of her sisters
that had attracted "Cupid" Amory most,
she persisted in making remarks to one and
all of their guests to the effect that she considered Mr. Amory was behaving shamefully
—trifling with the affections of both the
girls by a studious impartiality in his attentions, after having given each of them good
cause to suppose he meant something more
than flirtation. Theodora's almost fierce

denial, and May's tearful protestations, only
the more firmly convinced Anne that matters
had really gone too far in both quarters.
What was to be done? The man couldn't
be expected to marry them both, and, for the
matter of that, she heartily hoped they
would both refuse him, for Anne meant to
move henceforth in a higher social sphere, and
to have a brother-in-law whose grandfather
had been a doll's-eye manufacturer did not
at all fall in with her new views of life ; but
still the man ought to be made to propose ; it
wasn't to be supposed that he could play fast
and loose with any Brassingham, and then
shoot off to some other quarry just when
everybody was supposing he was on the
point of making an offer !

Thus argued Anne Brassingham, in the
loudest tones and in the most decided
manner, to all and any who had the time or
the inclination to listen to her. She spoke
to her father, but her father declined to
interfere. She told Vere that he ought to
take her brother's place, and plainly ask

young Amory his intentions, but Vere felt
he had enough on his hands already without
meddling in the love-affairs of his future
sisters. Anne would, doubtless, have taken
the young fellow to task herself, had she not
felt that any notice on her part would inevitably induce him to believe himself beloved,
and against this her family pride revolted.

Occupied as all the Brassinghams were
with affairs of their own, Mr. Brassingham
himself with Miss Champneys, Miss Lavinia
with the Rev. Silas Monckton, Anne with
Vere Vereker, and her sisters with "Cupid"
Amory, it would have fared ill with the
necessary arrangements for the wedding and
the fancy ball if Frank Freeman and Gerald
Tresilian had not been at hand to render
valuable assistance.

Freeman's wonderful powers of organization, and Tresilian's exquisite taste, found
full scope in planning, marshalling, and
adorning all available resources. Armed
with unlimited powers from Mr. Brassingham, these two young men, nominally acting

under the ladies' orders, took all the manage-
ment and trouble off their shoulders.

Mrs. Higgins's hopes of being included in
the festivities at Brassingham Park were
more than fulfilled.   Anne was not unmind-
ful of Miss Patty Higgins's services as
"gooseberry-picker," and Theodora's delight
in Agatha's society increased day by day as
the latter's noble and unselfish character proceeded to unfold itself to her.   Mrs. Tempest
and her daughter were popular with every
one, while Loftus Tempest and Captain
Selfe were put up with by the Brassinghams
for the sake of their belongings.

For the Brassinghams, taking people and
things very much on the surface, only saw
disadvantage to themselves in the society of
a disreputable *roué* and a still more disreputable tippler.   Partly their bringing up,
partly their own freedom from unfashionable
vices, partly that contempt for the weaknesses of others which so often defaces the
characters of those who enjoy sound and
perfect health, had made them, as a family,

intolerant of faults or vices that had no
temptation for their own natures. But the
influence of Agatha Bonchurch was gadually
unfolding a higher purpose in life to many
about her, and especially to Theodora Brassingham ; and Theodora, being the moving
spirit in the house, proved a valuable ally
in checking the roystering improprieties of
Selfe, and in hiding the shamed self-
consciousness of Loftus Tempest.

In Julian Ferrand, too, both Selfe and
Loftus had found a staunch friend. The
young giant had come to watch for his cue
from Agatha Bonchurch or Frank Freeman,
and where they led he was never slow to
follow. For, much as both these young
people delighted in the fresh vigour and
glorious strength and beauty of the Brassingham family, yet the deeper and stronger
feelings of both were reserved for the world's
halt and blind and sorrowful. The trouble
and affliction of their fellow-creatures attracted them both far more than their joys,
—in the case of Agatha Bonchurch from a

rare sense of sympathy, combined with the
highest acknowledgment of Christian duty;
in that of Frank Freeman from an acute
sympathy, too; but in him a humanitarian
philosophy took the place of religious obli-
gations, while his combative nature stimu-
lated him to the defence and upholding of
all who were the victims of their own or
others' ill-doing.

Such was the mental attitude of the
Brassingham family and its guests when
Mrs. Steele made her appearance at Bras-
singham Park.

CHAPTER XII.

CONCERNING THE BRASSINGHAM DIAMONDS.

THE advent of the new dressmaker was
hailed by all the ladies of the Brassingham
family with unfeigned delight. Neither the
Brassingham girls nor Miss Champneys were
clever with their needles, and though they
dressed well, it was to the taste of Madame
White they owed the fact and not to themselves. But Madame White could not be
supposed to superintend the thousand and
one frivolities necessary to so extensive a
trousseau as that of Miss Brassingham; her
working deputy had fallen ill with fever, of a
sort, too, that might—who knew?—be catch-
ing; and Miss Lavinia had sternly forbidden
any dresses from the infected household to

cross the threshold of Brassingham Park.
Therefore Mrs. Steele's assistance had
arrived in the nick of time.

Mrs. Steele was a born artiste. She had
been early apprenticed to one of the most
fashionable modistes in the London of her
generation, before the craze for the stage
had seized upon her. She had had immense
experience, in her theatrical career, in pro-
ducing startling effects out of the most un-
promising materials, and, now that she had
carte blanche to spend what she pleased, she
thoroughly delighted the young ladies by
her taste, intelligence, and originality. Her
grave reposeful manner was in itself a charm.
Her voice was low-pitched and sweet in
tone, her attitude towards the girls half-
respectful, half-motherly; thus it came to
pass that in a very few days from the time of
her arrival her advice was asked and her
opinion taken upon all sorts of subjects
foreign to her duties as a modiste.

Strange, indeed, to her was her position.
Five-and-twenty years ago she had nourished

the hope that John Brassingham's fierce passion for her would have made her mistress of this very mansion where she was now a hired servant. And now his daughters by another woman were grown to womanhood, while for one of them she was herself preparing the wedding dress. Strange, too, that the lawful heir should at this juncture be an outcast from his father's house, while Mr. Brassingham's eldest son—his son by her— should be a beloved and highly favoured guest.

Sadly and sorrowfully did the woman so long ago deserted contrast what was and what might have been, as she busied herself with the *trousseau* of the daughter of the woman who had filled the place she had once hoped to win; and perhaps she might win it yet, she would say to herself, if Violet were safely married to Julian and out of Mr. Brassingham's reach. Poor deluded woman! to think that her faded charms could ever now find favour in the eyes of a man like John Brassingham; or that moral rectitude or a late repentance would ever weigh one feather's weight in the scale against his passions or his self-indulgence! Yet hope against hope she did. To admit the possibility of failure was too dreadful a thought for brain to bear. She had loved him then in those early days when she had yielded to his seductive tones and vigorous beauty, she loved him even more now, even though his caresses had turned to aversion, and the maturity of his manhood was past. Ah! how had she fed on the memory of those three years of bliss, for which she had endured five-and-twenty years of exile. Could fate, indeed, be so cruel that her declining years must be passed in loneliness and abandonment after all she had gone through?

The large room that had been given up to her as a work-room was situated in that portion of the house which was especially set apart for the unmarried ladies of the family. There was little chance, therefore, of either Mr. Brassingham or Julian making

their appearance therein, but the girls were
in and out all day, and discussed all topics
freely before her.

Shortly after her arrival opportunity
gave her an insight into the feelings of
the family on the subject of the diamonds.

Anne was engaged in trying on various
articles of apparel in Mrs. Steele's work-room,
under that lady's immediate surveillance,
and her sisters had strolled in from their
own rooms to give their opinions on the
matter.

"Does any one know what is the matte
with papa?" asked May, when she had
criticized the fit of some half-dozen dresses.
"I asked him some trivial question just now
downstairs, and he almost swore at me."

"I have not seen him in such a passion
since the day he and Charlie smashed the
drawing-room furniture, and Charlie shook
the dust from his feet as he left the house,"
added Theodora. "Do you know, Anne,
what has upset him?"

"Oh, yes," answered Anne, with the air of an Amazon bored with tilting against windmills. "It is the old bone of contention—the diamonds, *my* diamonds. I mentioned casually this morning, after breakfast, that I meant to wear them in church, and that if papa was going up to town he might as well bring them back from the bank."

"And what did he say?" exclaimed both the sisters in a breath, while a pin that went rather deeply into the solid mass of Anne's body led her to rebuke the dressmaker's momentary awkwardness.

"Say? Oh he said much as usual when that topic is broached," said Anne, with a forced air of unconcern; "only he worked himself up into a much worse passion than before; said the diamonds were not mine, never had been mine, and that he was blessed if they ever should be mine, swore at me much as if he had been a navvy and I a navvy's daughter, and ended by informing me that, as the jewels were his, and his alone to dispose of, he intended to give them to Violet."

Another pin missed its legitimate course and imbedded itself in Anne's firm round arm.

"I really must ask you to be more careful, Mrs. Steele!" she cried. "My body is not a pincushion."

"I wish those wretched diamonds were at the bottom of the sea," observed May; "they have been a source of trouble all our lives."

"And before we were born, my dear, as Vere has lately found out," replied Anne. "It seems that papa gave them to some one else before he married mamma,—to some actress whom he admired, I believe; but Vere would not tell me the whole story, though of course we can all pretty well guess the real state of the case."

"But if the diamonds were given to this lady," said May, innocently, "how is it they ever came back to make more mischief?"

"I believe our grandfather got them out

of that *lady's* hands, May," said Anne, with
sneering emphasis, "by making her a handsome allowance if she would give up his
son and the diamonds at the same time."

" But you don't mean, Anne," asked May,
incredulously, and blushing to the roots of
her hair—"you don't mean—" and then she
came to a dead stop. Bright innocent May
could not bring herself to frame in words
the accusation that she felt was implied
against her father.

"Yes, I do mean," answered Anne, significantly; "and you may just as well hear the
truth from me as from any one else. Papa gave
the diamonds to some low creature who
danced breakdowns in spangles and tights."

"Stop, Anne!" said Theodora, her eyes
flashing furiously. "I won't hear papa run
down, or hear you blacken his character.
Doubtless papa had his faults, but this is not
the time to speak of them"; and she nodded
significantly towards the dressmaker, who
was busied in trying to make a dress meet
round Anne's not too slender waist.

"But about the diamonds," urged May, anxious to keep the peace between the sisters, a task which fell to her lot on an average about twice a day. "If they were bought back from the person you have spoken of, and if mamma had really no power to leave them to you, then it seems to me they must be heir-looms, and that Violet can only have them as a sort of loan, while she is papa's wife. I suppose they must go to Charlie some day, and be worn by his wife, and then to Charlie's son, and so on. Is not that the way with heir-looms generally?"

"Heir-looms, indeed!" said Anne, contemptuously. "As if we Brassinghams were likely to have heir-looms! You seem to forget, May, that our grandfather used to put his mark to a deed, because he couldn't even write; and if the jewels came into the family through a woman, as they undoubtedly did, there is no reason why women should not inherit them. Besides, Brassingham itself is not entailed. There is no property with which the jewels must necessarily go."

"But surely Charlie must be heir to Brassingham itself," suggested May, bent on getting at the bottom of the matter.

"Not at all," answered Anne; "Brassingham might be sold and divided between us girls; or it might be left to any one of us to the exclusion of the others; or it might not be left to us at all. Vere says we are a larger family than we were aware. Perhaps some of the brothers and sisters we have never seen may come in for the lion's share. Who knows?"

"For Heaven's sake, Anne, do hold your tongue!" cried Theodora, her dark face all ablaze with offended pride and disgust at her sister's obstinate hatred of their father. "Gracious! Mrs. Steele! are you ill?" she added, as the dressmaker, with something between a gasp and a sob, let drop her work, and fell fainting against the table.

"It is nothing," said Mrs. Steele, recovering herself. "The heat of the room, perhaps. I am not accustomed to much standing about."

May, always thoughtful and considerate, had rushed off to get some wine and her salts-bottle, and Theodora took the opportunity of impressing strongly upon Anne the folly and wickedness of unfolding to a mere child, just out of the school-room, the dark history of their father's younger days.

Further conversation, however, on the subject was stopped by May's return with the wine; and Mrs. Steele was soon restored to her usual equanimity.

At this juncture Miss Higgins's faint giggle was heard on the stairs, and shortly, accompanied by Agatha Bonchurch and Matilda Tempest, she made her appearance in the work-room.

"We left mamma and Mrs. Tempest at home," she said, as she entered, "unravelling a genealogical mystery, that a hundred years ago a Higgins married a Tempest, or a Tempest was step-mother's second cousin to a Higgins, or something equally involved and unintelligible; so, the subject not interesting us, we have come to inspect the *trousseau.* How are you getting on, Anne?"

" Oh, pretty well. The dinner-dresses are finished, and the ball-dresses nearly so, but I am in despair about the velvet morning costumes *en princesse.* They require to fit so exactly, and the trains are all too short; but Mrs. Steele is doing wonders in altering them. Do you think this mauve silk should be trimmed with lace, or with velvet of another shade? Velvet,—well yes, perhaps, as winter is coming on."

And so Anne rattled on, smoothing out this, testing the quality of that, enlarging upon the fineness of her cambric, the value of her furs, and the matchlessness of her lace, while her friend Miss Higgins duly admired and envied the endless paraphernalia that lay littered about the room.

CHAPTER XIII.

A WATER-PARTY.

"And what are the men doing with them-selves?" asked Anne, abruptly, as she proceeded to try on all her hats and bonnets for the satisfaction of her friend.

"Mr. Brassingham has taken Miss Champ-neys up to town in the mail phaeton," answered Matilda Tempest; "Captain Selfe, Mr. Ferrand, and Loftus, are playing pyramids in the billiard-room; Mr. Tresilian is arranging flowers in the hall, and Mr. Freeman is making out lists of all sorts of things in the study."

"Those two men were really invaluable," said Theodora, alluding to Freeman and

Tresilian. "They can do anything and everything on an occasion of this sort. Frank has written and sent all the invitations in papa's name; settled all the vexed questions of bridesmaids and groomsmen, processions and carriages, who is to take who in to church, out of church, and in to breakfast; who is to propose whose health, and who is to return thanks for the same. Yes; Frank is a genius on these occasions!"

"And Mr. Tresilian has turned head gardener," said May, "much to the disgust of the lawful lord of the flowers, fruits, and vegetables. Fancy! although there were four of us girls to look after the arrangement of the flowers, papa vows we never had a flower in the house until Mr. Tresilian came, and certainly never a vase properly filled."

"I don't know one flower from another," said Anne, as if she rather piqued herself upon her ignorance, "and Theodora is more at home in the stables than in the garden. May has had her lessons to learn, and her music to practise, and Violet has been occu-

pied ever since she came in listening to
somebody or other's love ditties, so it's just
as well that the men in the house should
do our work, though, for my part, I think
messing about with note-scribbling and the
arrangement of flowers is a very effeminate
line for either of them to take up."

"Grateful creature!" exclaimed Theodora,
bridling. "How beautifully you have banged
all our heads together with one sweep of your
indiscriminating satire! If Frank has the
bump of method largely developed, and Mr.
Tresilian a fine artistic taste, why should
they not use them without being considered
effeminate?"

But Anne, having parted with all her
available venom in her last biting speech,
only shrugged her shoulders, and declined
to argue.

"We want to make up a party to go on
the river this afternoon," said Miss Higgins.
"Who feels inclined to come?"

"What men are included in 'we'?"
asked Anne, in her nastiest manner. "You

should let us see how your lines are baited, Patty."

All the girls looked uncomfortable, as Anne intended they should. Theodora tossed her head after the usual fashion of an indignant Brassingham, and May became unbecomingly hot with blushing.

"It is Mr. Amory's suggestion," said Agatha Bonchurch, quietly. "We met him on our way through the Park, and he has ridden down to Mortlake to see about a boat. Miss Higgins and I have promised to go; Miss Tempest does not like the water. Mr. Tempest is going, I believe; and there will be room for four more, if four can be found to venture."

"Oh, Theodora and May had better go," said Anne. "For my part I hate the water. But you must get some more men; only two men to take care of four ladies will never do. Besides, Eric Amory is no use in case of accidents. He can't swim. Can Mr. Tempest swim?"

"Not well enough to be of much use to

other people," said Matilda Tempest, smiling; "but an accident is hardly possible in a 'tub.' They do not mean to venture in an outrigger."

"Theodora will have to save the lot," said May. "She can swim like a fish and dive like an otter."

"Well, we need not meet the devil halfway," said Miss Higgins. "Let us hope Miss Brassingham's powers will not be put in requisition. In the mean time let us go down and try to persuade some more men to come."

Thereupon the girls stormed the billiardroom, where Tempest, Selfe, and Ferrand were playing pyramids, but they took no captives. Tempest had said before that he would go. Wherever Agatha Bonchurch went he was sure to follow. But Selfe had promised to return to Barnes to drive Mrs. Tempest to Richmond, and Ferrand had planned a long ride across country with Frank Freeman. Mr. Tresilian, too, was obdurate. Theodora said he was afraid of spoiling his clothes, May thought him incapable of handling an oar, and Agatha knew, though she concealed her knowledge, that he was too desperately afraid of Miss Higgins's advances to join any party of which she might form one.

So, on Amory's return, the two younger Misses Brassingham, Miss Higgins, and Miss Bonchurch, were, with Loftus Tempest, all that could be found to join the water-party.

It was arranged that the party should walk to the river.

Eric Amory, with more decision than usually characterized his actions, attached himself resolutely to May. Agatha manœuvred so that Loftus Tempest should bear Miss Higgins company, and herself brought up the rear with Theodora.

The friendship inaugurated at the Yorkshire Wells between Agatha Bonchurch and Theodora Brassingham had steadily and fruitfully increased. Each felt respect and admiration for a character so opposed to her

own, and yet so noble, generous, and trustworthy in itself.

But Agatha, beyond other feeling for her
friend, had a deep pity for the great heart
that she knew had given itself to Eric
Amory, and given itself in vain. As an
intelligent outsider Agatha rightly gauged
Eric Amory's affections. His admiration
was for Theodora, but his heart was
May's. His nature was inclined to lean
upon another; there was more of the ivy
than the oak about him, and this led him
to appeal continually to Theodora's sound
judgment and strong good sense whenever
his own failed him, which was not seldom;
but he was withal rather afraid of her, and
would conceal much of his more childish
thoughts from her, which to May he was
wont to blurt out without reserve. In short,
Eric Amory felt Theodora's superiority and
resented it. What can be more fatal to love
than this? But in Theodora's mind, apart
from the all-absorbing passion of love, inspired by the boy's blue eyes and golden

curls, there was a deep, deep yearning at her heart to raise him to a higher moral and mental sphere. Personally, he was a god to her already, but a god of her human passions, not of her loftiest imaginings. Perfect peace to her must be the realization of the first, combined with the strongest hope of making him the last by her own constant love and example.

Truly he was the most beautiful being the eyes of Theodora had ever dwelt upon, as he strode on by May's side with that long swinging stride of his, so full of grace and power. And Agatha, watching her and divining her thoughts, could not repress an involuntary sigh. What had Theodora done that so heavy a disappointment should be hers?

Long before now had Theodora unburdened her heart of its hopes and fears to her friend Agatha; but what help could be given her? To suffer nobly was all that was left her, and Agatha could but enlarge upon the uses of suffering and the mysteries

of pain in endeavouring to apply some heal-
ing balm to a wounded heart, hurt with a
wound for which she knew no cure.

"What a picture those two make, side by
by side, Agatha," said Theodora, as they
followed the rest through the Park. "Youth,
beauty, wealth, and love, all will be theirs,
and so much more of each than falls to the
lot of most mortals; and yet, were May any
one else than May, how fiercely I should
hate her!"

"Yet May being May," replied Agatha,
"you can love her all the more that
she is beloved by him. Is it not so,
Theodora?"

"I hope it will be so, Agatha. My prayers
and my will daily wrestle with my love that
it shall be so; but there is no love without
jealousy, and my love is too vast to allow
my jealousy to die all at once, even though
I feel and know that he has chosen May
before me. Oh, Agatha, how shall I bear
it! I have loved him so passionately, so
very, very dearly. Ever since we were but

children he has been to me as a young god!"

"My poor friend, take heart," said Agatha, soothingly. "Oh, that I could instil into you some of that faith in God's providence that makes life bearable to me. Depend upon it, Theodora, the time will come when you will see God's hand in all your misery, as the hand of an all-wise and loving Father."

"I am not a religious woman," said Theodora bluntly; "and I cannot accept comfort in which I do not believe. If I could believe with you, that Providence shapes the affairs of man, I might be more content, at any rate more resigned; but Frank Freeman has fixed the ideas and beliefs that have always been floating hazily in my brain, and I no more than he can find comfort in the hope of supernatural interference with our mortal joys or pains."

Agatha sighed deeply. "Mr. Freeman has much to answer for," she said; "for myself, the trials of life would be insupportable but for the daily, hourly strength I draw from communion with the Unseen. But apart from religion and its consolations, Theodora, remember that 'all things come to them who know how to wait.'"

"To them who know how to wait!" echoed Theodora with dreary scorn. "How should waiting bring me my love? It would be bad enough to continue to love a man who became another woman's husband; but that one should love one's sister's husband,—oh, Agatha!"

"Theodora," said Agatha, gently but gravely, "you are a girl with strength of mind and firmness of purpose; there are but two courses open to you,—you must either marry Eric Amory yourself, or root out this passion from your heart, and destroy it utterly. There is no middle course. I should be no true friend to let you believe there is. Tell me, are you sure, quite sure that it is May he loves, not you?"

"Quite, quite sure," answered Theodora, in so broken a tone as left no doubt on

Agatha's mind of the sincerity of the speaker. " Quite sure," she repeated, drearily; "for I was strolling down the south shrubbery yesterday just at dusk, taking some bread to the swans on the mere, and thinking how all this was to end. When I reached the great mountain-ash by the broken palings at the end of the shrubbery (you know the tree I mean) I sat down and —and had a good cry. On the other side of the palings there is another seat — the mountain-ash overshadows both—and while I was drying my eyes, and taking myself to task for being such a weak fool as to give way, I heard his voice—Eric's voice—on the other side of the palings; I looked through the broken wood; there he sat with his arm round May, her head on his shoulder, his lips on her cheek, while he poured out all his love for her, and asked her to be his wife. And I heard her answer; saw all the glorious rapture of love mount to her face, and shine through her eyes; saw him press his lips on hers and linger there in silent joy. How I bore it I don't know; but I am glad I did bear it. I am even glad I did see it, for the agony of uncertainty was becoming intolerable—worse, I think, than even the dull knowledge that my future is made desolate."

The two girls, as they talked, had fallen far behind the rest of the party, for the footsteps of sorrow are lagging.

"My poor, poor friend!" said Agatha, as she drew Theodora to her warm embrace. "Would that I could help you bear your trial!"

Then they sat down together at the edge of Brassingham Park, and mingled their tears in silence, Theodora weeping for the death of her life, in that she might love her love no longer, and Agatha for very sympathy.

"But has May not told you?" said Agatha, as they resumed their walk. "Surely she owed it you to tell you first of all."

"I heard Eric say he wished his mother to hear it first from his own lips. She is away for a few days, so he asked May to say no word of their engagement, even to papa, until to-night, when Lady Amory will return. He thought his mother would be hurt if any one knew his happiness before herself."

"But surely May knew how much you cared for Eric, Theodora. Was she content to accept him without one thought of you or of your misery?"

Theodora flushed painfully. "You and I do not place the same value on truth, Agatha dear," she said. "You know I am of opinion that the expression or repression of truth should wait upon judgment and reason; you think judgment and reason should be the slaves of truth."

"Mr. Freeman's teaching again," burst out Agatha, interrupting her. "Oh, Theodora! beware of his plausible sophistries."

"Frank Freeman has doubtless done much to set my crude thoughts, Agatha, but the germs of these opinions were my own from the earliest times in which I began to think.

But never mind that now ; my reason for saying anything on the subject was to excuse myself for doing what I know you, from your point of view, would consider wrong— I deceived May as to my real feelings for Eric."

"Oh, Theodora, that was wrong indeed ! Expediency can never be an excuse for deception."

"Our minds are finite," said Theodora, sententiously, "and truth, to a finite mind, can but be comparative. But to return : May loved Eric. She had told me so. Of course I have known it all along. Still, she did tell me so, and she could not take back her confidence. But I know May well enough to be sure that, had she thought her happiness could only be purchased by my misery, she would have renounced Eric then and there, even if Eric had not transferred his love from May to me. Therefore, I lied to May. I say 'lied,' because I feel *you* would say my deception was a lie. I told her my love for Eric was as a sister for a

brother, almost as a mother for a son. If
May had been older she would not have
believed me; but she is only seventeen,
and has not learnt to know by signs
what she cannot find out by words. Therefore it was that she accepted Eric's love
without qualm of conscience on my account."

The girls' *tête-à-tête* was here interrupted
by Loftus Tempest and Miss Higgins, who
had come back to see if anything was the
matter, so long had they lagged behind. It
was not long before they reached the boat-
house, where Eric and May had been some
time waiting.

Though the day was bright and sunny, a
stiff breeze was blowing from the south-east,
and the water was "choppy." Even in a
"tub pair" the motion was unpleasant.
They had come for a row, however, and a
row they would have. So the ladies sat as
cosily as possible in the stern, while Eric
and Loftus took the oars. The Brassinghams were accustomed to the river, but Miss
Higgins and Agatha Bonchurch began to

feel uncomfortable as they neared the Ship at Mortlake, and begged to be put ashore.

This necessitated the disembarkation of the whole party, for the girls could not well walk alone along the towing-path to Putney while the men took back the boat. After some little discussion it was suggested that the boat should be sent back by a boatman from the Mortlake boat-house, and that the party should make a short cut home through Barnes and Roehampton on foot. But Eric seemed vexed at having come so far only to go home again, and proposed to race Loftus Tempest in canoes, while the ladies should stand as umpires on the bank.

Tempest, however, had never been in a canoe in his life, and, not being able to swim well, had the good sense to decline Eric's offer.

CHAPTER XIV.

THEODORA PADDLES HER OWN CANOE.

THEODORA, however, with the combative instincts of her race, could not see a glove thrown down without taking up the challenge.

"I will race you," said she to Eric, "and Mr. Tempest shall escort the rest along the bank. The man who takes the boat to Putney can bring back the canoes."

"All right," said Eric. "What shall it be for—a dozen of gloves?"

"Four-buttoned if you lose," assented Theodora, laughing; and she settled herself in her canoe.

Whatever Theodora did she did well.

She handled her paddle with skill, and soon she and Eric were in position in midstream.

"Isn't it very dangerous?" said Miss Higgins, with her usual giggle.

"Oh, Theodora knows how to take care of herself," said May. "She has paddled her own canoe, in more ways than one, ever since she was born."

"But the current is running so strong, and the water is so choppy," urged Agatha. "Do you really think it is safe, Mr. Tempest?"

But, before Tempest could reply, May had said, "One, two, three, and away!" and the canoes were rushing towards Putney with the tide, which had begun to ebb; and May, followed at intervals by the others, was tearing along the towing-path, waving her handkerchief at the rival boats.

Theodora was ahead, and was making the distance greater at each sweep of her paddles. She had looked round in saucy triumph once or twice at her pursuer, and was now going steadily down stream, looking straight ahead of her, when a cry from May on the bank caused her to look sharply round.   Eric and his canoe had disappeared.   The two halves of his broken paddle floated past her on the stream.

And Eric could not swim!   The full sense of the situation flashed on her like lightning.   A bend of the river had hidden the accident from all but May, who with childish delight had bounded on in front, keeping pace with the canoes.   In his eagerness to overtake Theodora, Eric had put forth a strength disproportioned to his skill or the toughness of the paddle.   The sudden snap had made him lose his balance, and the boat had filled on the instant and gone down.

May stood shrieking on the bank.   Loftus and the others were still at various distances behind, while a bed of willows still shut them out from view.

Pale as death, but with perfect self-control, Theodora backed her canoe almost to the

spot where the circles still eddied round
where the boat had sunk, and peered into
the water for some sign of Eric. But the
current was strong, and had swept him
further out into mid-stream, and carried him
further down the river.

A moment more and she saw an arm and
a lock of golden hair. That moment was
enough. Theodora threw herself out of her
canoe and struck out strongly for the spot
where the dear head had again gone down.

As May had said, Theodora could swim
like a fish and dive like an otter. Immediately above the spot where Eric had sunk
the second time, Theodora dived, found
Eric, and grasped him by his golden hair.
Fortunately for them both, he was too far
gone to struggle. Slowly, bravely, sturdily,
Theodora made her way to the bank, striking
out with all her force with her right arm
alone, while in her left hand she clutched
Eric's golden curls. As she neared the
towing-path she felt her strength failing.
She could not see, and there was the hum

of rushing waters in her ears. But help was near. Loftus, unable to swim himself, had reached the spot breathless, just as Theodora's strength had failed and by wading up to his neck had caught them both before the current had carried them out again from the shallows. May's screams had been heard even at the Ship, and people who knew what to do were already on the spot, to help the terrified group, only one grade less helpless than the half-drowned pair themselves.

Theodora was only exhausted—exhausted to such an extent that she was happily insensible to the wild anguish of May, who believed that her darling, her Eric, had been drowned before her eyes.

Eric for a long time showed no signs of life. The kindly boatmen tried all known means of restoring suspended animation, but for a while, which seemed to the terror-stricken onlookers an eternity, all efforts were unavailing. The bright, gay face was livid, the swollen eyelids closed.

At last, with a sort of low, broken sigh, life returned in a fitful spark to Eric Amory. There was another sigh, then a gasp, then a quivering palpitation of the limbs; and a sense of hope, dim, but yet possible, thawed the ice-bound hearts of the circle who watched him with such agonized intensity.

Theodora, who by this time had somewhat recovered under Agatha's care and the absorption of stimulants, had raised herself from her prone position to her hands and knees, and was bending over the livid countenance of Eric Amory with an anguish terrible to witness. All were too intent upon Eric, however, to notice her emotion. Only when an old boatman, who had been foremost in his endeavours at resuscitation, remarked cheerily, "Thank the Lord! he will come round now!" did nature refuse to respond to the cry of joy where she had boldly borne the wail of sorrow, and Theodora fell forward in a dead faint as Eric opened his blue eyes once more to the light of life and love.

They carried both of them back to the
Ship at Mortlake. A messenger was
despatched to Brassingham to bring back
the carriage immediately, and another for
the nearest medical man.

Eric lay in a sort of stupor in the bay
window of the Ship. They had cut his wet
clothes off him, and wrapped him in heated
blankets. He lay dreamily conscious of
what was passing round him, and even returned the pressure of May's hand; but he
had not spoken nor moved, and the girl's
terror was not removed.

Upstairs, above him, lay Theodora. Faint
followed faint. No sooner had she come to
than nature sank again, and she was uncon-
scious as one who was dead.

Slowly, very slowly, however, both Eric
and Theodora came round. Each had such
a splendid fund of vitality, such force of
vigour, such a strong hold on life, as defied
the onslaught of the destroying element.

By the time the carriage arrived, with
Anne alone inside, almost beside herself with

anxiety and alarm, both Eric and Theodora
were respectively half-dressed in such warm
clothing as could be supplied to them by the
good people of the Ship, and were capable of
being lifted into the carriage and conveyed
to Brassingham Park, whither they were
soon followed by the rest of the party in any
vehicles that came to hand.

The doctor, who had arrived just as the
carriage drove up to the Ship, allayed
Anne's exaggerated fears.

"The worst was past," he said. "Nature
would pull them through." However, he
accompanied them back to Brassingham, and
stayed with them until the return of Mr.
Brassingham, who had taken Violet to
London to choose her wedding dress.

Hard as Anne's character was at ordinary
times, illness or danger brought out all her
best points. She had been her mother's
nurse, companion, and friend for years, and
in the commotion and terror caused by this
boating accident, she showed herself an able
and gentle woman, as well as a thorough

Brassingham. Mr. Brassingham absent, and
Theodora placed *hors de combat*, there was
no one, it is true, who could interfere with
Miss Brassingham's ways of doing things.
But her ways were good ways when she had
the opportunity of planning, arranging, and
carrying out the work she had in hand
without having to encounter the opposition
of the rest of her family. In an emergency
like the present, Anne Brassingham showed
at her best; and Agatha, who, after narrowly
watching her for months, had come to the
conclusion that nothing would rouse her
from her indolence, coldness, obstinacy and
selfishness, was absolutely amazed at the
tenderness, the forethought, and the powers
of organization that a sudden crash had
brought to light in a woman usually so
stolidly indifferent to all that went on
around her.

Lady Amory was to arrive at her own
house at six o'clock. Anne sent a carriage
to bring her on at once to Brassingham
Park. A man on horseback was despatched

along the London road to hurry Mr. Brassingham and Violet to all possible speed; while Anne herself—the phlegmatic, indolent, unwieldy Anne—was in and out of every room in the house, ordering, advising, consulting, expostulating, as if she had for the first time in her life woke up to a lively sense of her own conscious individuality.

Dinner was not till seven. Mr. Brassingham and Violet were not expected till that hour. Vere was in town on lawyers' business, and Tresilian had accompanied him to be witness to some deeds. Selfe and Miss Tempest had returned to Barnes to drive with Mrs. Tempest and Mrs. Higgins to Richmond; and Frank Freeman and Julian Ferrand had gone for a long ride across country to Willesden, and would not be back till dark. So for many hours the majority of the guests were in ignorance of Eric's and Theodora's misadventure.

CHAPTER XV.

FERRAND AND FREEMAN.

Soon after Eric Amory and those of his party had gone on the river excursion that had ended so unfortunately, and well-nigh fatally to "Cupid" himself, Frank Freeman and Julian Ferrand had trotted down the broad smooth carriage-road that led from house to lodge of Brassingham Park, and had then struck across country to Hammersmith Bridge. This crossed, they passed some way down Hammersmith High Street, and, turning to the right, took the road to Acton, by the side of which a long reach of turf for a couple of miles gave them the opportunity of freely exercising their hor es.

Through Acton and along the main road, with its small neat terraces of suburban cottages, they went, till where the ground begins to rise towards the heights of Harrow-on-the-Hill. Here they paused.

Said Freeman, "If we go across country here to the south-west, I think we shall about strike Kew Bridge, and get home by Richmond Park and Roehampton. That will be better than returning by the way we came, and will not take us longer than the time we have till dinner."

Said Ferrand, "I do not know the country at all, but I am ready to follow wherever you lead."

"It must be somewhere in this part of the world," said Freeman, as he reined his horse alongside of Ferrand, "that Miss Champneys must have had that extraordinary adventure of which Mr. Brassingham has told us. I wonder the girl had the courage to allow herself to be blindfolded, and taken off, goodness knows where, by an old woman whose face even she was not allowed to see!"

"It was on the principle of love casting out fear, I presume," answered Ferrand, rather grimly.

"Miss Champneys's conduct is perfectly inexplicable to me," resumed Freeman. "I have known her now for more than two years. She has none of the vices of the girl of the period. She does not care for position, or money, or display. She has not much pride and no vanity; yet here she is, deliberately marrying a man, handsome enough, it is true, but old enough to be her father."

"Miss Champneys is of a gentle, clinging nature," observed Ferrand, his swarthy, sunburnt face grown grave with the pain of his passion; "and I think gratitude plays a larger part in her character than any other quality whatever. Her duty, as she understands duty, to those who are kind to her, overwhelms all other considerations—"

"Except love," interrupted Freeman. "To do Miss Champneys justice, I believe she would have thrown all other considera-

tions to the winds had Charlie been true to
her. Only when love deserted her did she
listen to the suggestions of gratitude, and,
perhaps, expediency."

"Not expediency," said Ferrand, hesitat-
ingly, for as yet he had not confided to
Freeman the proposal he had himself made
to Violet.

"Well, yes, I should say expediency,"
continued the other; "for, you see, it was
quite impossible for Miss Champneys to go
on living under the care of her avowed lover,
unless she became that lover's wife; and,
penniless as she is, the bait was a large one
—to become mistress of Brassingham Park,
instead of going out into the world as a
governess."

"There has not been occasion for her
to choose between such extremes," said
Ferrand, hoarsely.

Freeman looked up at him, and saw that
the hot blood had rushed over his cheeks
and brow, and a fierce gloomy fire was in
his great black eyes.

"Why, how do you know?" he asked; though in his own mind he had answered his own question before Ferrand could reply.

"Because I proposed to her myself," Ferrand answered shortly. "That is how I know."

"Forgive me, my dear fellow!" said Freeman. "Of course I suspected that you had been attracted by Miss Champneys at the 'Wells.' One could not help seeing it, and others saw it too; but I had no idea that matters had gone so far as this. I have pained you, Ferrand, by my remarks. Forgive me! I did not know."

"There is nothing to forgive. I ought to have told you, perhaps, before," returned Ferrand; "but one is loth to speak of one's disappointments in love, and I did love her with all my heart and soul and mind and strength."

"Well, old fellow, I confess I am surprised. I don't want to flatter you, but if I had been a girl I don't think I should have

looked twice at Mr. Brassingham if you had
been in the way." And he ran his eye over
the young man's magnificent proportions
with a critical glance of open admiration.

"Men's ideas on such subjects are not
women's," said Ferrand. "Because you
have paid me the compliment of setting me
on a pedestal for anatomical criticism is no
reason that I should find favour in the eyes
of a young girl; besides, apart from that,
her mind's eye was filled at the time with
the person of Charles Brassingham, and I
have been politely given to understand by
Miss Theodora that I am but a lout compared
to her brother. Tell me, what is this young
gentleman like?"

"Well, you know Charlie Brassingham is
a great pal of mine," said Freeman; "and
I am apt to let my enthusiasm colour my
favourites. He is a fine-looking fellow, and as
strong as a young bull; much handsomer, to
my thinking, for a man, than his sisters are
for women. Anne is too massive for feminine
beauty; Theodora too dark and on too large

a scale, and, though I admit May is a perfect
picture, yet she is but a picture, and lacks
the vivacity and variety of real flesh and
blood—at least, so it seems to me. But
Charlie has the best points of all the girls;
May's Greuze-like colouring and bright
brown hair, Theodora's vigorous frame and
intellectual expression, and the massiveness,
which in Anne is unwieldy, forms the
very perfection of what a man's figure
should be.

"By Jove!" ejaculated Ferrand, "you
are indeed an enthusiast, Freeman! To
satisfy human nature's laws he should have a
flaw somewhere in his list of perfections.
Surely he squints or limps, or has a club-foot,
or is pitted with small-pox? Come now,
relieve my jealousy by a few of his imper-
fections."

Freeman laughed. "Physically I can see
no imperfection in him; but then, as I told
you, I am enthusiastic about personal
beauty. The lack of it in my own case has
made me give it undue importance, doubt-

less, in my estimate of others. No, do not
interrupt me," he added, as Ferrand opened
his lips to disallow his companion's verdict
against himself; "I used to be chaffed as a
boy about my ugliness—yes, that was the
word—ugliness; at seventeen, the age when
one is most sensitive as to one's personal
appearance, my own mother told me, half
laughing, half sighing, that it was better to
_be honest than good-looking, by which she
meant that she endorsed the verdict of my
schoolfellows; and if a man's own mother
thinks him plain, what must be the opinion
of outsiders? In short, throughout my
youth I was always given to understand that
my appearance was against me while
strength and good looks were the only
standards by which youth judged youth of
both sexes. The conviction of my short-
comings did not embitter me, but my reason
has not been balanced enough to stem the
universal torrent of homage paid to external
perfections; on the contrary, I have out-
stripped the mob in my admiration for form

and colour and proportion, and have become, as an artist, a worse idolater than the vulgar herd."

"You look a man, a proper man, every inch," said Ferrand. "What can you want more? I hate to hear you depreciate yourself, as you have a habit of doing. I do not say that it is mock modesty in you, for I see that you unfortunately really believe what you say; nor do I accuse you of affectation, as I think many would, to hear you undervalue your own proficiencies; but I do think, my dear fellow, if you will not be offended by my friendly criticism, that you betray a self-consciousness that is nearly akin to vanity, and that an intellect such as yours should strive to prevent such betrayal."

Frank Freeman winced under this home-thrust. He felt it was true, yet he strove to defend himself.

"My dear fellow," said he, with rather a forced laugh, "it is all very well for you, from your vantage ground of gigantic height and strength, to pat my five foot ten on the back, and say, ' Cheer up, my little man, the race is not always to the swift, nor the battle to the strong,' which is what I know you would say, only you think it might wound me ; but in my experience the race is to the swift, and the battle is to the strong. I hate proverbs ; they aim at such exact truth, such pithy precision, that they generally fly as wide of the mark as lies, with, what is worse than lies, a plausible morality countenanced by quasi-experience and tradition, as if there were not two sides even to a proverb. I admit I am self-conscious. What then ? It does not follow, surely, that I should be conceited ? ''

" I did not say conceited, I said vain," interrupted Ferrand ; " there is a wide distinction between the two."

" A distinction without a difference in such a case as this," urged his friend. " I am self-conscious, because throughout my youth my inferiority to others was forced down my throat by all with whom I came in contact. I was considered plain even to ugliness, weakly almost to effeminacy, dull to the verge of stupidity."

"And have come to maturity," interrupted Ferrand, "vigorous, manly, and intellectual."

"I asked myself, years ago," added Freeman, taking no notice of the other's complimentary parenthesis, "whether such were really my characteristics. I found that I was ugly, but I knew I was not effeminate, and I hoped I was not dull. Since then my whole life has been an effort to excel intellectually, to counterbalance, as it were, my physical inferiority to my fellows."

"Frank Freeman, excuse my bluntness, but you are now talking d—d nonsense. You are vigorous and brimming over with health, and there is hardly an accomplishment in which you have not far distanced every one of our own age. If you go on depreciating yourself, I shall begin to think you are only fishing for compliments, which you won't get from me; so let us return to our muttons, so to speak. You have not

satisfied the cravings of my jealousy by
telling me of Charles Brassingham's short-
comings. I am dying to glut my soul with
them—so proceed."

"He is not so tall as you by some three
inches," said Freeman, thus adjured; "nor
is he so big-boned. Again, he is ruddy and
blue-eyed, while you are swarthy and your
eyes are black; yet there is something about
you both which is strangely alike. I think
it is that you both have a manner that com-
bines a caress with a threat, an entreaty
with a defiance, a look that says, 'Obey me
for affection's sake first; but I'll knock your
head off if you do not obey me at all.' I
know that manner and look go down with
all women, and—and with some men! I
wish to goodness I knew the trick of them
both!"

"Well! you have not said much in
Charles Brassingham's disfavour, yet," said
Ferrand, smiling at this hero-worshipper,
in spite of himself, "unless it is that he
possesses some vague resemblance to your

humble servant; but I want to know some worse traits in his appearance and character even than that."

" Well, then ; if I must abuse him," said Freeman, driven to bay, " he is a Brassingham ! You have seen the family character— faults and foibles, follies and vices, attractions and virtues ; Charles Brassingham is an epitome of them all, good, bad, and indifferent. He is brave as a lion, generous to a fault, but obstinate, hot-headed, and violent ; he is extravagant and sensuous, rather coarse, a trifle dull, and has not any brains to spare. Now have I extinguished your jealousy ? There is certainly nothing heroic in such a character as I have drawn of Charles Brassingham."

" There is not," said Ferrand, quietly, but with a certain grimness ; " for you have accurately portrayed myself ! "

" To leave the subject of Charlie's character for a moment, Ferrand," said Freeman, " I am afraid I have proved a bad guide. I thought this lane would have brought us out

about a mile to the north of Kew Bridge.
We are really not far from Brentford End;
but I see no outlet to the main road. We
must get across this field and that patch of
common yonder. We may have to take a
fence or two, but our nags do not seem
tired."

The lane had ended in what once had
been a small morass; but the dryness of
the weather had turned the ground into
lumps of grit and clay, while rushes and
rank grass rose in tufts between the stones.

As Freeman spoke, his horse placed his
foot on a treacherous mass of dried mud and
flints, slipped, stumbled, and fell. Before
Freeman could extricate himself the horse
rolled over upon him. A stake, driven into
the mud when the soil had been soft, had
been broken off short about a foot from the
ground; its jagged edge being concealed by
a tuft of rushes. On this Freeman had fallen,
and the weight of his horse falling upon him,
drove the stake into his side, tearing the
flesh from the ribs to the spine. He lay

immovable, with closed eyes, the blood satu-
rating his clothing as he lay. His horse
struggled to his feet almost as soon as he
had fallen, but his master made no movement.

"Heavens! Are you hurt?" exclaimed
Ferrand, as he sprang from his horse. Then,
when he saw the closed eyes and ashy pallor
of his friend, the full gravity of the accident
dawned upon him. Close by was a bank of
grass, sheltered by bushes of wild sloe and
briar. With the tenderness of a woman and
the strength of a giant did Ferrand carry
his friend in his arms across the sun-dried
lumps of soil and the tangled grass. Then,
laying him on the bank, he tore open his
coat and vest, and strove to staunch the
blood that flowed freely from the jagged and
gaping wound.

"Great heavens! the man will bleed to
death!" cried Ferrand in an agony. He
sprang to the top of the bank and shouted
for help. On the other side of the briars
he perceived a tiny rivulet, so small as to

have escaped observation hitherto; but carrying a good draught of water in its narrow bed. Hastily he filled his hat, and dipped his handkerchief in the stream, then shouted again at the top of his stentorian lungs, and sprang back over the hedge to where Freeman lay.

He dashed the water on his brow, moistened his hands, washed the blood from the wound, and bound the wet rags about it as best he could. Thank Heaven! a footstep! Nearer and nearer it came. He looked up and saw a woman coming rapidly towards him down the lane; a tall, majestic woman, very simply clad, very young and fair. He shouted again, beckoned and pointed to the bank and the prostrate figure lying there. She began to run. In a moment she was by his side. There was no need for words. She saw what had happened at a glance. Gently she bathed Freeman's forehead, rapidly and skilfully she changed the bandages, as each blood-stained kerchief was washed in the running stream. In silence for some time they laboured, those two, Ferrand rinsing the linen, she binding up the wound.

At last she spoke.

" The flow of blood has stopped," she said. " The last bandage is not stained. Help me to bind this silk round him, without moving him, or the wound will start afresh."

As she spoke she disengaged from her neck a long silken scarf, and bound it tightly round the sufferer's waist.

Freeman moaned.

" Thank God!" exclaimed Ferrand and the fair-haired girl in a breath. " Then he is not dead!"

They moistened his lips with water. He opened his eyes and moaned again. The girl glanced up at Ferrand's colossal figure standing over her and the wounded man.

" You look as if you could ride straight," she said. " We must get more help at once. There is but one house hereabouts—my uncle's; his name is Ferris. Do you see yonder clump of firs? Ride straight for them, on the further side of the house; but you will have to jump the garden fence about a hundred yards from the courtyard. It is high, on the top of a steep bank. Remember you cannot take it flying. Tell them to come at once, and bring some trap— whatever is at hand—round by Love Lane and the Willesden road ? But let some one come back with you. I will wait here and mind him. Bring back some brandy. Say you left him with Alice Graves."

Smartly as she rapped out each minute instruction, there was no hurry in her manner, no perceptible excitement. Her tone was decided and resonant.

No feeble character was this; and so Ferrand felt as he sprang on his horse, and rode straight for the clump of firs.

CHAPTER XVI.

"WHEN GREEK MEETS GREEK, THEN COMES THE TUG OF WAR."

Now it happened that Mr. Charles Brassingham, whose humble friends kept him well supplied with news of all that was going on at his father's house, had been much exercised in his mind all day by the last bulletin—namely, that Violet had been taken that morning to London by his father to order her wedding dress. In a very turbulent and wrathful humour he was parading the grounds at the back of Ferris's house, when he saw a horseman making his way straight across country, without the slightest regard for the agricultural products of Mr. Ferris's best-farmed fields.

Young Brassingham had had several rows with such horsemen on this same subject since he had accepted the hospitality of Mr. Ferris's house, and as he saw Ferrand coming tearing up to the very fence at the end of the garden, as though he would clear it clean, his anger rose to real Brassingham pitch, and he shouted out, in very unparliamentary language, that he would break the stranger's head if he did not instantly turn back.

Ferrand, intent on his mission, feeling that haste was necessary and damage justified in a cause of life and death, put his horse at the ditch on the near side of the bank, jumped it, and scrambled up to the hedge on the top, when a grasp of iron was laid on his bridle, and his horse, even in mid career, forced back on his haunches to the imminent risk of breaking his own and his rider's back.

The bank was broad at the top, and the sudden jerk at the bridle had made the animal swerve violently on one side, which saved it from slipping back into the ditch in the rear.

The blood mounted furiously to Ferrand's face. The motive of his trespass was lost for a moment in the surging passion that almost choked him, as he shouted—

"D—n you, for an insolent fool! Let go my bridle!"

"D—n you, for another!" retorted Brassingham, to the full as furious as his opponent; and he forced the horse closer to the outside edge of the bank.

Down came Ferrand's heavy hunting-whip on the hand that held the bridle. With the savage yell of some wild animal, Brassingham, furious with rage and pain, sprang at him, caught him round the neck, and, in a moment, men and horse were floundering in a heap in the ditch at the bottom of the bank.

"When Greek meets Greek then comes the tug of war." The horse, with a wild plunge, regained his feet, and, snorting with terror, started off across the field, his bridle trailing on the ground.

Sudden as the shock had been, crushed as both men were by the weight of the animal, neither lost his hold on the other for a moment. They had struggled into a standing position, too closely intertwined for blows. Shoulder to shoulder, knee to knee, they rocked and strained, and rocked again. With every muscle tense, with teeth close clenched and starting eyes, each strove to wrench himself free from the other's herculean grasp and hurl his opponent to the ground; all to no purpose. Like a rock each stood, yet neither could free a hand to strike, so tightly interlaced were their sinewy limbs. As they stood glaring, furious, speechless, hugged in each other's fierce embrace, two figures sprang upon the bank—two towering men, no whit inferior to the two below. With one bound they were upon the exhausted combatants, and had wrenched them far apart.

They were the ex-prizefighter and his nephew George.

There was a moment's pause. Almost

spent, bruised, and shaken as both Brassingham and Ferrand were, their eyes gleamed
with no abated fury; but all idea of closing
again must perforce be abandoned with the
two Ferrises' stalwart frames between them.

Ferrand first found voice to speak.

" Take no notice of this," he panted. " A
man lies dying yonder, half a mile beyond
the firs; a girl is with him. She sent me
here for help. She said her name was Alice
Graves."

Like a lightning flash the lowering faces
of the three men changed.

" Why the devil couldn't you have said so
before?" said young Brassingham, sullenly;
but he hung his head.

" There is no time for words," said Ferrand, hurriedly. " Alice Graves said help
would be given if I used her name. My
friend is dying, perhaps is already dead.
Brandy is wanted, and a trap. He was
speechless when I left him. He has lost
much blood. There is no time to lose. She
said—the girl who is tending him—' Send a

trap round by Love Lane and the Willesden
road, and bring some one back with you
direct the way you go.' My friend lies at
the end of a narrow lane which ends in a
dried-up bog. Who will go back with
me?"

"I will," said Brassingham, promptly,
flashing his blue eyes meaningly into Ferrand's face, and holding out his hand.

"All right," said Ferrand, as he took the
proffered hand ; and even as he wrung it, all
the savagery died out of his great black
eyes, and a gleam of real honest admiration
shone in them instead.

"I think you and I shall be friends, young
sir," he said, gravely, and he still held young
Brassingham's hand.

"I am quite sure of it," replied the other.
"Your horse has gone. We must saddle two
of our own."

"They are saddled already," said Dick
Ferris; "George and I have but just dismounted. We saw the horse gallop riderless
across the field, and came to see what was

up, and not much too soon either," he added,
grimly.

"The brandy, uncle; get the brandy,"
cried George Ferris, as they rushed into the
courtyard. "I will take round the trap; you
see to a bed being got ready, and send for
the nearest doctor. Cavey is in the house;
he can dash into Brentford on the
mare."

The brandy was brought and a bundle of
linen rags. In a minute more Julian Ferrand and Charles Brassingham, ignorant of
their relationship, of their rivalry, even of
each other's names, were scudding across
country to where Frank Freeman was lying
sore wounded, but still alive.

He was in a sitting posture when they
reached him, his dark-grey eyes wide open,
his head supported on the bosom of Alice
Graves. Very white and weak he looked,
but a faint smile flickered over his face as he
recognized Charles Brassingham.

That young man's surprise and concern
cannot be described, as he found in the

wounded stranger no other than the friend
and companion of so many years.

"My poor dear old fellow!" he exclaimed, as he sprang from his horse and
rushed to Frank Freeman's side. "To
think that we should meet again like this!"

"The brandy! where is the brandy?"
said the practical Alice. "Can't you see he
is faint from loss of blood?"

Freeman was revived speedily by the
stimulant. An amused look stole into his
eyes as he regarded Julian and Charles
Brassingham standing in front of him side
by side.

"So you have introduced yourselves!"
he said, in a very low weak voice.

Charlie Brassingham coloured, and was
silent; but Ferrand linked his arm into that
of his late antagonist as if they were old
friends, and said, with a cordial ring in his
voice,—

"We have, and very heartily too!"

Then they looked at each other and
laughed.

"A common danger makes a quick intimacy," said Charlie, by way of explaining the situation.

"And a mutual sympathy makes fast friends," added Julian.

Freeman glanced from one to the other inquisitively. The young fellows' faces were flushed and heated, and there was a merry twinkle in their eyes he could not understand.

"Why, where on earth have you met before?" he asked.

"Never; and we don't know one another's names even now," said Ferrand.

Freeman's countenance fell. Alice saw his change of expression, and held up a warning finger. "You must not let him talk," she said, "he is too weak; give him some more brandy. How long will they be with the trap?"

"George started with it while we were waiting for the brandy," said Charlie. "He cannot be long now. How do you feel now, old fellow?" he added, turning to Frank Freeman.

"I am not in much pain," he answered; "but I feel too weak to move."

"I think we shall be able to tackle you between us," said Charlie, laughing, as his eyes met Julian's; "if not, there is another little boy coming who will give us a helping hand."

Freeman's face lighted up with admiration at the two magnificent young fellows before him, and he remarked that he thought, perhaps, a pair of such young giants might prove equal to the occasion.

There was a rattle of wheels; a light trap was coming as quickly towards them as the ruts and lumps of mud and tufts of rushes would allow.

"Hulloa! Stop, George!" shouted young Brassingham, holding up his hand. "Go back and wait at the end of the lane. He cannot drive over such ground as this. It will shake the life out of him."

He turned to lift Frank in his sturdy arms; but he found himself forestalled.

Gently, tenderly, had Ferrand taken Freeman in his arms, and was already striding
along the rugged lane.

" Whatever have you two been about?"
said Alice, as she, for the first time, caught
sight of a back view of both the young men.
" Why, your clothes are in ribbons, Charles,
and so are that other gentleman's. Were
you both spilt on your way? I gave you
at least credit for being able to keep your
seat; and he looks as though he could take
a tight grip of his animal!"

" Ah, that cursed bank!" said Brassingham, flushing and laughing. " By Jove!
our appearance is rather ragged. But go
you and settle his cushions, Alice, while I
untether the cattle and bring them along."

Alice did as she was bid. The hind part
of the trap was a sort of small waggonette,
the seats being placed sideways opposite
each other.

" He will do best on the floor," said she,
as she arranged multitudinous cushions and
rugs George had thoughtfully flung into the

body of the trap before starting. "You
had best ride back with Mr. Brassingham,
sir, and I will mind the gentleman. There
will not be room for you."

Mr. Brassingham! The truth dawned on
Ferrand for the first time, and the shock
was great. This young athlete, then, the
only man he had ever met who could hold
his own against him in sheer physical
strength, was the man whom Violet loved;
his—Ferrand's—successful rival, John Brassingham's outlawed son! As he swiftly put
two and two together in his mind, he won-
dered the truth had not flashed on him
before. He laid Freeman tenderly down on
the floor of the trap. It drove slowly away.
He turned to meet his antagonist, his rival,
his friend now, and, though still unknown to
him as such, his brother, Charles Brassingham.

Violent as were Julian Ferrand's passions,
turbulent as was his nature, combative as
were his instincts, yet his generosity was
above them all. He loved Violet Champ-

neys with all the great strength of his strong nature, actively at first, when he believed her free to be wooed and won; then passively, but none the less strongly, when he found her the affianced wife of a man whom he knew in his heart she could not love; and now—now that he had seen the bright beauty, the magnificent vigour and strength and pluck of the man who had first loved her, and been loved by her in return, a sickening feeling of defeat and jealousy passed for a moment over his soul, to give way the next moment to a, nobler, more generous sentiment, self-repressing, self-denying, as he swore to himself by the great love he bore her that he would strive to reunite her to the real idol of her heart.

CHAPTER XVII.

THE RIVALS.

His mind once made up, Julian Ferrand cast out all jealousy as unworthy both of himself and of the woman he loved.

As soon as he had mounted, he turned to his companion, with a look half superior, half admiring, as the difference in their years and their recent encounter instinctively suggested.

"You are, then, Mr. Charles Brassingham, I presume," he began; "at least I think I cannot be wrong, from the remarks let fall by Miss Graves."

"I am that vagabond," answered Charlie, laughing, "'homeless, ragged, and tanned,

who so contented as I?'" and he carolled forth
the lines blithely in a full, deep baritone.
" And who are you ? "

" My name is Julian Ferrand. I am at
present staying with a Mrs. Higgins at
Barnes, who is, I believe, a friend of your
father's; at any rate I know she is an intimate acquaintance."

" Ah ! I have heard of you often," said
Charlie, somewhat shortly. " I hear of most
people who are much at my father's house.
He has got the house full at present for my
sister's wedding, has he not ? "

" Mr. Vereker's uncle and aunts are there,
and, of course, Mr. Vereker himself, and a
Mr. Tresilian, who is to be Vereker's best
man, and your friend Freeman. Those are
all at present; but I heard this morning that
all Mrs. Higgins's household, including the
Tempests, Captain Selfe, and me, were to
take up our quarters at Brassingham Park
until after the wedding is over. I believe
the visit is to begin from to-morrow."

" The devil it is ! " said Charlie, rather

rudely. "Anybody else coming to-morrow as well?"

"Lady Amory and her son, I believe," said Ferrand. "I have not heard that any one else is expected." Then suddenly and earnestly he leaned over in his saddle to the bright, handsome young fellow at his side, and said, "But surely you will be there too? You cannot think how your sisters miss you, and others besides your sisters even more."

Charlie flushed crimson, and darted a quick glance at the speaker. "Is the man chaffing me?" thought he. No; there was no satire in the grave, swarthy face, only a great look of kind concern, of subtle sympathy, which disarmed Charlie's suspicions in a moment, and made him feel he could trust this man through thick and thin.

"Ah, you know all about it, then," he said, still blushing like a girl.

"Yes, I know all about it," answered the other, dreamily. "I'm awfully sorry for you, Brassingham. I feel as if I had no right to speak, but believe me I am your friend."

"I don't doubt it," said the other, warmly. "I don't know much, but I can tell a good fellow when I see one, and a false man from a true."

"May I speak my mind, then?" said Ferrand.

"As much as you please; only don't expect me to come home again."

"That is just what I do expect you to do."

"Then we had better talk of something else, for I never mean to set foot in that— in my governor's house again," said Charlie, relapsing into sullenness.

"Look here, Brassingham," said Ferrand, with that grave emphasis of his which always compelled people's attention, whether they would or no. "Some instinct compels me to speak out, and I cannot let the opportunity slip by. I know Miss Champneys well, better than you think."

Charlie's blue eyes flashed up at him suspiciously.

"She is devoted to you, body and soul. She loved you first, and has loved you all along, but by all accounts—may I speak out?"

"Yes," said Charlie, impatiently, "but what?"

"By all accounts you have not been equally true to her."

"Not true to her! Why, by all the powers, I have never looked at another woman since I asked Violet to be my wife! Who says I have not been true to her?"

"She saw it with her own eyes," said Ferrand, gravely. "When you had that final interview with her at Brassingham Park, did she not tell you as much herself?"

"She said more; she swore she had seen me on my knees to another woman, and my head in that woman's lap."

"And was it not true?"

"True!" shouted young Brassingham, the hot flush of anger dyeing his face. "Now by all the gods this is too much! True! I swear it was not true. I swore it was not true to her, and she would not believe me; therefore I left her, therefore I leave her now. I have my faults, but I am not a liar. Come, now, do you believe me?" and he shook his head back with the haughty air so familiar to Violet herself.

The youth's bold face was crimson with anger and excitement. His fierce blue eyes glittered as he turned to Ferrand, waiting for his reply.

"I do believe you, Brassingham," said Ferrand, simply and gravely. "There has been some great misunderstanding, if, indeed, there has not been foul play. Of this, however, I am certain, that Miss Champneys really believes she saw you, and will continue to believe so, unless you can prove that it was not the case."

"How the devil am I to prove I was not Tom, Dick, or Jerry on his knees to Tom's, Dick's, or Jerry's sweetheart?" said Charlie. "I don't even know where she saw this young gentleman who is given to laying his head in his mistresses' laps."

"Nor do I," said Ferrand; "but she would doubtless have told you herself if you had asked her; and I suspect your father and our friend Freeman must have some knowledge, or at least suspicion, of the truth, as far at least as Miss Champneys knows it herself. You must remember she was blindfolded during the whole drive, and cannot even state positively in what direction the carriage took her. A hoax there has been, but I cannot readily divine its object. Have you any idea on the subject? Who could have benefited by the rupture of your engagement with Miss Champneys?"

"Nobody but the governor, that I know of," responded Charlie, promptly. "But though he and I have had many a row, he would rather die than take a mean advantage of any man, even in the field of love."

"Here we are at your gate, or rather at your friend's," said Ferrand. "By the way, what is the name of the owner of the house? Graves, I presume, as that is the name of the young lady who came to Freeman's assistance."

"No; the house belongs to a man of the name of Ferris. The young fellow who brought the trap is his nephew, and is engaged to Alice Graves, who is the niece of Ferris's wife. Curious coincidence, isn't it? Ferris and Ferrand! There are lots of Ferrises about, I believe, though not related to these people; but I never knew any one else called Ferrand but yourself."

Ferrand had dismounted, and was standing, bridle in hand, waiting for one of the stable helps to take his horse. At Brassingham's last words Ferrand started as if he had been shot.

"Merciful Heavens!" he burst out, and then he suddenly stopped and stood openmouthed, gazing wildly at Brassingham. He had suddenly remembered his promise to his mother not to betray his relationship to her until he had heard from or seen her again; and here he was (there could be no doubt whatever of the truth) actually stand-

ing on the threshold of his uncle's house.
while his own brother would be there in a
few minutes, and their common history
would be known to Brassingham, to Freeman, and through them to all at Brassingham
Park. All this and much more flashed
through Ferrand's brain in a moment.
What was to be done? True, his brother
had heard no name, and ten years had as
effectually changed his own appearance as it
had that of his brother. He could not leave
Freeman between life and death in a strange
house; he could not avoid meeting George
nor old Richard Ferris, who, when he heard
his name was Julian Ferrand, could hardly
fail to recognize his sister's son. That
honesty is the best policy had always been
Ferrand's line of morals, and he determined
hastily to abide by it now.

"Why what the deuce is the matter?"
said Brassingham, astounded. "You look
as if you had seen a ghost."

"The matter!" said Ferrand, with a
forced laugh. "Why, a ghost is a joke to

this! This young George Ferris is my own
brother, whom I have not seen for ten
years past, and the old man is my mother's
brother!"

"But your name is Ferrand," said
Charlie, more and more amazed at the turn
affairs were taking.

"True; I have lived all my life abroad;
my mother chose to slightly change her
name, and I, living always with her, adopted
the French form of Ferris, as she had done.
But George was adopted by my uncle, and
kept to his right name."

"Well, this beats cock-fighting — I'm
blessed if it doesn't!" said Charlie. "I feel
rather dazed, Ferrand; but here comes
George, with poor old Frank and Alice.
By Jove! it's like the last scene of a melo-
drama at the Adelphi. Slow music and blue
flame. Recognition of the long-lost brother.
Stage embrace. Sensation. Curtain!"

"Hush! For Heaven's sake don't say a
word yet! Let us get Freeman safely into
the house, and not disturb him with a scene.

George will not recognize me with this black beard. As soon as Freeman is safely housed and attended to I will speak to George; and now, silence. Here they are!"

The jolting of the waggonette, even carefully driven as it had been, had proved too much for Freeman. He had fainted again. Scarcely, however, had he been laid upon a couch within the house, in that great central hall where Violet had seen, or believed she had seen, her happiness melt away for ever, when the doctor's gig drove up to the door, with William Cavey at the doctor's side.

"It was a bad wound," the doctor said, "but there was no danger to life. The jagged stump had lacerated the nerves at the base of the spine, but the spine itself was quite uninjured. The patient must be kept in one position till the wound had healed, and must rest from all exercise for some time to come."

Mrs. Ferris looked up in dismay. If

Freeman were to be nursed in her house, the whole Brassingham party would be for ever about the place—a circumstance not to be thought of for a moment for many more reasons than one.

Mrs. Ferris was a woman of promptitude and decision. She made up her mind that at all hazards Frank Freeman must be taken back to Brassingham Park.

She drew the doctor aside. "This is most unfortunate," she said. "I may appear inhospitable, but it is quite impossible for us to take this young gentleman in. Every room in the house is engaged; and besides, I am loth to undertake the responsibility."

"Rest easy, madam," said the doctor. ,, I shall sew the wound up, and apply an astringent lotion that will effectually stay the bleeding. Let Mr. Freeman have a little soup and wine, and in a very short time he can be taken back to Brassingham Park."

Mrs. Ferris was mightily relieved. She

bustled about, getting the wine and soup, while Alice Graves, who was a born nurse, acted as the doctor's assistant in binding up and bandaging the wounded man.

CHAPTER XVIII.

FERRAND AND FERRIS.

GEORGE FERRIS had taken the trap round
to the stables, and thither, as soon as Freeman's wants were attended to, he was
followed by Julian Ferrand. The latter had
been too much occupied, first by his fierce
struggle with Charles Brassingham, and
afterwards in arranging the interior of the
waggonette for Freeman's comfort, to notice
what manner of man his brother had become
in the ten years that had elapsed since he
had last seen him.

In the shadow of the coach-house, Julian
saw a young man leaning against the steps
of the waggonette.

"Charles Brassingham again!" said he to himself. "I thought I had left him indoors. However, he will tell me where my brother is."

He advanced across the courtyard. "Will you tell me where to find—" he began; then he stopped short. It was Charles Brassingham, surely. He could not be mistaken in that clean build, those massive shoulders, that smooth square chin and brown moustache; and yet there was something—

The young man looked up. Instead of the flashing blue eyes of Charles Brassingham, a pair of large dark eyes, bold and brown, met his astonished gaze.

Ferrand stood irresolute—puzzled. This was Charles Brassingham, and it was not! The young fellow saw his hesitation.

"Can I do anything for you?" he said, advancing from the shadow of the coachhouse, and standing right in the blaze of the then setting sun.

"I thought it was Brassingham!" said Ferrand, as he saw now a difference in the expression of the mouth, and heard a difference in the tone of voice to Charlie's. "Is it possible that you are—?" and then he stopped again, for he felt it was impossible that this could really be his brother.

"My name is George Ferris," said the other, reddening under Julian's earnest gaze. "Brassingham and I are thought much alike."

The brothers had been all in all to one another in their boyish days, as two boys bereft of most other ties will be.

A glow spread over Julian's swarthy face; he extended both his hands, — "George, dear old fellow, I am your brother Julian."

George stared at him a moment in infinite amaze, then, with a cry of joyful recognition, he threw himself into his brother's arms. Then, as his English training reminded him of the proper coldness due to their age and sex, he held Julian at arms' length by both hands.

"My dear old fellow, to think I should have you with me once again!" he said. "Do you remember how —?" and then he linked his arm in Julian's, and rambled off into all the sweet reminiscences of boyhood, the days before fate had parted them.

In happy memories, in mutual admiration and astonishment, in interchange of hopes and fears, and what news each might have to tell, a swift hour had flown by, when Charles Brassingham came out from the house to say Freeman was ready to undertake the homeward journey, and to see how the long-parted brothers fared.

Truth to tell, young Brassingham was almost as excited at this strange conjuncture as either Julian or George. Throughout his long friendship with the latter, the virtues and prowess of the former had been so dinned into his ears by George that he had a double reason now for entering into the triple alliance these three so cordially formed.

They found the invalid much refreshed by food, stimulant, and the doctor's skill. Pale, very pale he was certainly, but the pain was eased, and the faintness had quite passed off.

The old prize-fighter suggested that a pair of horses would go smoother than one, so another carriage of the break description, which was kept more for picnic parties than anything else, was brought out of the coach-house, and speedily got ready.

Alice Graves would not be parted from her charge until she had seen him safely into other female hands, and Charles Brassingham consented to go as far as the avenue of limes that skirted one side of his father's house, rather than leave Frank Freeman in his present weak condition.

The break was large and roomy; Freeman was laid along one side, Charles Brassingham and Alice Graves balanced him on the opposite seat, while Julian mounted to the box-seat next his brother. Freeman's face was towards the horses, that the evening breeze might refresh him; a groom had been ordered to take his horse and Ferrand's over to the Park the following day.

In the hurry and excitement of meeting Julian, and preparing for Freeman's com-

forts, George Ferris had found no opportunity of introducing his brother to his
uncle or his uncle's wife, and Alice Graves
was too thoroughly occupied with the sick
man to open up any communication with
her as to the last strange event of this event-
ful day. So they departed on their way,
leaving the older Ferrises ignorant of who
the young stranger was, and marvelling
much at the sudden intimacy that had
sprung up between him and George.

Ferrand himself felt that now was not the
time for explanations. Not even Freeman
had any idea of the relationship of the
brothers, and for reasons of his own Ferrand
preferred that a day or two should be
allowed to elapse before Mr. Brassingham
was informed that one of the wedding
guests was but the nephew of a retired prize-
fighter, who now kept a public-house, half
farmhouse, half inn, not many miles from
Mr. Brassingham's very gates.

CHAPTER XIX.

ALICE GRAVES RETURNS MISS CHAMPNEYS'S CALL.

THE break rolled slowly and smoothly along the London road, over Hammersmith Bridge and along the road to Barnes Common. Near Roehampton, the London road through Putney to Richmond joins the one along which George Ferris's pair was being quietly driven. Suddenly a mail-phaeton and pair of high-stepping bays whirled past them, coming round a corner behind them so sharply as almost to lock in the break's hind wheels.

The driver of the mail-phaeton whipped up his off horse, and left a bare inch between

the traps in passing, but he did not touch
the break, and there was no jar or damage.
The lady by his side took a quick glance
at the occupants of the further side of the
break, and disclosed to Charles Brassingham
the lovely and beloved features of Violet
Champneys.

For an instant only Violet's lovely eyes
swept over the man she loved and the fair
large woman sitting by his side. To Charles
Brassingham it was but a chance meeting,
an unfortunate rencontre, which brought the
flush to his cheek and the flash to his blue
eyes; but to Violet it meant much more.
She had seen again, close to her beloved,
that same fair woman on whose lap she had
before seen his curly head in the large hall
of some house, she knew not where. What
further proof was needed? He was still true
to her hated rival. Bah! she would pluck.
the gay deceiver from her heart.

There was a tightening of the coral lips,
a sudden blanching of the damask cheeks;
but she did not look round again, and in

another moment the mail-phaeton was far ahead, with a cloud of dust between.

Mr. Brassingham, for it was he who was driving, had been too much occupied with steering clear of the break to notice any of its occupants, and Violet, one may be sure, kept silent as to what and whom she had just seen.

He was late. It was already getting dark; the bays were given the rein, and dashed home at a spanking pace.

Poor Violet sat mute till they reached the hall door. She let Mr. Brassingham lift her down, and crossed the hall with a stately gait. Then she rushed upstairs to her own room and threw herself on her bed in a wild agony of tears.

Julian, of course, had descried the Brassingham horses and carriage, and had seen the backs of Violet and Mr. Brassingham as the mail-phaeton whirled away before him; but on every account he had held his peace, and had not even looked round at Charlie to see if he too was aware who had passed.

When the break reached the avenue of
limes, Charlie Brassingham got out, said
hopeful adieux to Frank, and started to
walk back to Hammersmith, where he would
await George and Alice on their return.

The rest drove up to the hall door. The
brothers got down. George went to the
horses' heads, Julian entered the house to
tell the news.

Those who had composed the water party
had not returned to Barnes. A message had
been sent to state what had occurred; Miss
Higgins stayed to be of use to Anne; Agatha
to watch by Theodora, and Loftus Tempest
because the others stayed.

When Ferrand had told his news, all those
who were downstairs pressed into the hall.
"What a day of accidents this had been!
Where was it going to end?" Mr. Brassingham was dressing for dinner, and Violet
was in her room, May was with Eric, cha-
peroned by aunt Lavinia, and Anne was
watching by Theodora's bed. Vere Vereker
and Tresilian, Tempest and Miss Higgins

accompanied Ferrand to the hall door;
Agatha had rushed away to ask Anne what
had best be done. As she returned with
the acting mistress of the house, she caught
sight of Freeman's white face as he lay in
Ferrand's powerful arms while being carried
across the hall. Her own face whitened;
there was a thrill of concern, of anxiety, of
pity at her heart as Freeman's grey eyes
met hers; and we all know pity is near akin
to love.

"Can you carry him to his own room?"
said Anne to Ferrand. Then she looked
about for help. Her eye fell on Agatha's
white face. In the hurry and excitement
of illness and danger Anne's wits were
sharpened. She instantly divined what was
the disturbing cause in Agatha's breast, and,
turning to her, said eagerly,—

"Would you mind seeing to Frank,
Agatha? I feel half dazed by all that has
occurred. You had best take this young
woman with you," she added, as her eye
lighted on Alice Graves standing just within

the doors—"she seems to have been head nurse till now. I will come to you as soon as I can."

Then Agatha spoke to Alice Graves, and the two followed Ferrand and his burden up to Freeman's room.

And Violet, unhappy little Violet, where was she? Straining her eyes from her open casement above the entrance-hall, hearing voices and confusion, and the champ of the horses' bits, and the tread of many feet on the stairs; but not daring, with her red and swollen eyes, to come out to ask the cause of all this wild commotion.

The darkness had now closed in; Violet could just distinguish the break she had passed on Barnes Common. She saw the dim shapes of the horses, and the figure of a man standing at their heads, and that figure was very like her Charlie. With hands clasped and streaming eyes she watched him from her window.

"Oh, my love! my love! my love!" was her constant smothered moan.

She saw him intent on loosening the curb, which was chafing the near horse's mouth; a sudden light shot from the hall, revealing his face and form; but his eyes were veiled, and his head bent, and his face half turned away. But she had seen enough to leave no doubt upon a mind already influenced by all that had gone before. She cowered down in her agony, and hid her face in her hands.

A sharp knock at her door made her spring to her feet. The knock was repeated, and she heard Agatha's voice asking for admittance in tones that betokened hurry. She unfastened the door; Agatha stood without, and behind her Alice Graves.

"Water,—have you any water?" said Agatha, in breathless haste. "Those servants have not filled the jugs, and Mr. Freeman has fainted again."

She snatched the jug from Violet's hands, and rushed back across the passage to Freeman's room.

A sudden thought inspired Violet. Quick

as lightning she arrested Alice, as she was turning to follow Agatha, and dragged her across the room to the open window.

" Do you see that man ? " she gasped, her face white and drawn with anguish; " there at the horse's heads! As you are a woman, with a woman's heart in your bosom, tell me truly what is that man to you ? "

Alice, half terrified by her violence, half amazed, peered out into the darkness. Violet's eyes were riveted upon her face. The light in the hall glowed full upon the man. It was George Ferris.

" He is my affianced husband," she said, with mingled dignity and simplicity. " We are to be married in a month."

Violet did not cry nor faint.

" Thank you. That's all I want to know," she said; " you will find Miss Bonchurch in Mr. Freeman's room."

Frightened, perplexed, *jealous* for the first time, Alice Graves went out and closed the door.

Violet fell all of a heap on the floor.

How long she remained thus she did not know. She had not fainted, she was only stunned. Her senses were benumbed, for the last flickering hope of her life had flared in the socket and expired.

Presently she got up and lighted a candle in a mechanical sort of way. She went to the door. There was a hum of many voices in the hall. She looked out. The family doctor was passing down the stairs, and Mr. Brassingham was talking to him as he went.

" There is no cause for alarm," she heard the doctor say. " Your daughter is suffering from exhaustion and chill. She will be well in a day or two. Mr. Amory is young and strong ; the day after to-morrow will see him about again."

" And Mr. Freeman ?—you do not think badly of him ? " asked Mr. Brassingham, anxiously.

" There is nothing to fear at present," said the doctor, guardedly. " The wound is a nasty one, but it is only a flesh wound, and will soon heal ; but the nerves of the back are lacerated. It may be years before he recovers his old strength, especially his strength of nerve; but he is young and vigorous. With care all will be well."

"Should I telegraph for Lady Catherine?" asked Mr. Brassingham; "or will a letter do?"

"Oh, no need to telegraph; certainly not," said the doctor, cheerily. "If I mistake not he has a nurse who is quite fit to take a mother's place;" and he smiled meaningly.

"Which?" said Mr. Brassingham. "I did not notice anything."

"Ah! where are your eyes, Mr. Brassingham? Why, the dark one, to be sure; the girl with the Eastern face and the lithe Eastern figure. She looks very foreign. May I ask who she is?"

"She is a Miss Bonchurch, a Miss Agatha Bonchurch," answered Mr. Brassingham. "You surprise me; but I shall be pleased if it is true. They are both great favourites of mine."

Then the family doctor, that most privileged of dear friends where he is a friend at all, winked hard at Mr. Brassingham.

"The air of this house is aflame with love," he said. "It is burning in every room I have entered, and in some I have not been into. The more the better, my dear sir; and God bless you all!"

Then the doctor took his departure, and Mr. Brassingham, somewhat puzzled, joined the party in the dining-room.

Violet came down to dinner; for even the possessors of broken hearts must eat. Very pale she looked, but very calm. The worst was over now. Certainty was almost better than suspense. Love had proved false, but life is long. She would make the best of life. Dinner, as may be imagined, proved somewhat of a picnic. People came in and out, took a mouthful, added their mite to the disjointed conversation, and carried off tit-bits to the invalids. People ate by relays, talked by relays, nursed by relays. To all the terror and anxiety of an hour ago had succeeded a congratulatory chatter on the safety of the various invalids.

George and Alice had declined all hospitality, and had driven home, George in high spirits at having met his idolized brother, on whose prowess and pluck and strength he proceeded to descant in glowing terms to his companion the whole way home; Alice, silent and miserable, the canker-worm of a baseless jealousy secretly gnawing at her heart. But she would not, could not ask him to explain. No; her faith in her lover had been too implicit, her confidence too unbounded, her love too deep, for this. Besides, she did not even know the name of the girl whose conduct had sown these seeds of trouble in her mind, and, to accuse him of a *liaison* with a nameless lady—in Mr. Brassingham's house too, where she was sure George had never been before—would be really too absurd.

The idea of his having been mistaken for Charles Brassingham did not occur to her. Others saw a strong likeness between the

two, but Alice had seen them daily side by
side, and likenesses are never strong to those
of one's own household.

As may be imagined, there was no dearth
of subjects for conversation at the Brassingham dinner-table. Eric's narrow escape,
Theodora's heroic rescue, Frank Freeman's
terrible accident, were themes that occupied
every tongue.

An oft-repeated question was—Would
Anne's wedding have to be put off? But
Mr. Brassingham had "interviewed" the
doctor on this point, and the answer was
unhesitatingly, "No."

"But it is only a week now to the
wedding-day!" urged aunt Lavinia.

"Dr. Broadmead warrants the invalids
well in three days," said Mr. Brassingham;
"at least, Eric and Theodora in that time;
and he says Frank will be able to be at the
wedding, but he will not be able to dance at
the fancy ball."

"Have you telegraphed to Lady Catherine?" asked Anne.

"No, and I don't mean to," said her father. "A telegram would frighten her to death. I shall write to-night and make as light of it as possible. She will be here the day after to-morrow."

"Do you not think we ought to have a skilled nurse for Frank?" asked Anne, thoughtfully. "You see, his wound wants dressing continually, and we are all so inexperienced."

"Who dressed it before Dr. Broadmead came?" asked Mr. Brassingham. "I hate hired nurses about the place; they are sure to drink brandy from night till morning. Is no one of you girls equal to the occasion?"

"Agatha is better than twenty hired nurses," said Miss Higgins, putting in her oar. "She has had months of practice in a London hospital."

"But, my dear," said aunt Lavinia, severely, "Miss Bonchurch cannot sit up with the young man alone all night."

"I'll sit up with her," said Miss Higgins, promptly, "if that will satisfy propriety."

Aunt Lavinia shook her head.

"Lady Catherine is the proper person," said she; "and, till she arrives, a respectable woman of a certain age."

"My dear Lavinia," interposed Mr. Brassingham, "don't be absurd. These old-fashioned prejudices are out of place in so great a confusion. We must, for once, lay aside conventionalities."

"My first duty is to Theodora," said aunt Lavinia, "or I would sit up with him myself."

"It is not a matter of sitting up, Lavinia," answered Mr. Brassingham; "of course Ferrand or I or Tempest here are game for that; but none of us has any surgical skill, and that is what Miss Bonchurch has got."

"I think I can help in this," said Miss Elizabeth Vereker, who, with her sister and brother, had just entered the room. "I am old enough to be Mr. Freeman's mother, and I have had a deal of nursing in my time. Here is Miss Bonchurch coming down the stairs; let us see if she will accept me as her aide-de-camp."

Agatha, though unable to conceal a tell-tale blush, accepted both the patient and the assistant nurse. Lady Amory was expected every moment, and it was surmisable by most of those present who would share with her the watches of the night.

Anne, whose latent good feeling always came out in times of suffering, insisted on sharing with Miss Lavinia the nursing of Theodora; and so these weighty points were settled to the mutual satisfaction of every one concerned.

The staircase for the rest of the evening was a veritable Jacob's ladder. In any other household such a concurrence of misfortunes would have almost broken down both the domestic machinery and the family spirit. Not so with the Brassinghams. Their vigour concealed as ample a reserve force as would have sufficed for ten times the call made upon them, and though Lady Amory's hysterical anxiety, on her arrival, proved trying

to the already over-taxed nervous powers
of the womankind, yet the practical good
sense of the majority soon reduced her
to composure and allayed her maternal
fears.

END OF VOL. II.

LONDON:

PRINTED BY E. J FRANCIS AND CO.

TOOK'S COURT AND WINE OFFICE COURT, E.C.

www.ingramcontent.com/pod-product-compliance
Lightning Source LLC
Chambersburg PA
CBHW031422020726
47499CB00005B/1558